perfectly
ridiculous

Books by Kristin Billerbeck

Perfectly Dateless

Perfectly Invisible

Perfectly Ridiculous

perfectly ridiculous

A Universally Misunderstood Novel

kristin billerbeck

a division of Baker Publishing Group
Grand Rapids, Michigan

Published by Revell
a division of Baker Publishing Group
P.O. Box 6287, Grand Rapids, MI 49516-6287
www.revellbooks.com

Printed in the United States of America

Library of Congress Cataloging-in-Publication Data
Billerbeck, Kristin.
Perfectly ridiculous : a Universally misunderstood novel / Kristin Billerbeck.
p. cm.
Summary: Travel plans go awry when St. James Christian Academy graduate Daisy Crispin and her best friend Claire journey to Buenos Aires for a pre-college, pampering vacation.
ISBN 978-0-8007-1974-6 (pbk.)
[1. Buenos Aires (Argentina)—Fiction. 2. Vacations—Fiction. 3. Dating (Social customs)—Fiction. 4. Christian life—Fiction.] I. Title.
PZ7.B4945Pi 2012
[Fic]—dc23 2012003551

Published in association with the literary agency of Alive Communications, Inc., 7680 Goddard Street, Suite 200, Colorado Springs, CO 80920, www.alivecommunications.com.

12 13 14 15 16 17 18 7 6 5 4 3 2 1

To my sixteen-year-old self and anyone resembling her. You are God's beloved. Make sure any guy you're interested in treats you well. If he doesn't, move on before your heart gets too involved . . . so you will never feel "perfectly ridiculous." It's not your job to fix someone—only God can do that. So if a relationship makes you feel bad most of the time, that's not God's will for your life. Enjoy the world around you and your friendships to the full.

1

June 20

Fun factoid of the day: Abraham Lincoln never graduated from high school. He seemed to do all right for himself.

This was supposed to be my first travel journal. Travel! As in away from home and the rules and the stifling closeness of five people living in such a small house, which is covered with craft supplies and love, as my mom likes to say. This would be my first vacation, really, unless you count the time I went with my parents on that tour of Civil War battlefields—and I don't count that. Somehow I thought I'd feel different after graduation. Fulfilled, maybe? Accomplished? Something! High school was heinous, an insidious evil forced upon society's youth under the guise of education. (My best friend Claire and I made that up when we had to use insidious as a vocabulary word—nice, huh?)

Granted, high school is better if one is acne-free, can afford Forever 21 clothes, and manages to nab a boyfriend. Sadly, I was not one of those girls. I was the one who was good at math, wore homemade clothes, and had to work every day after school, while the wealthy kids at my private high school hung out at their country clubs. My mother claims this was character building, but by my calculations, I should be as big as Mickey Mouse when it comes to character. I was the nerdy girl who cute boys talked to only if they needed tutoring help or a lab partner.

I possessed none of the accessories that improve one's stock price in high school. At least, not until the bitter end when I managed to get a date for prom—sort of. (I was actually there doing community service—long story—but I did get one dance, and I told myself I could live on that.)

Naturally, no one will remember the bitter end. No, reality says they are going to recall the sum total of my high school experience and be surprised when I show up at our reunion in a store-bought dress. I know it's wrong to find my worth in what others think of me, or in material goods—my mother has told me so since birth, I believe. However, my mother also buys upholstery fabric to make her own dresses. She claims it has more structure and works like a built-in girdle. I think it just makes her look like furniture.

I've tried to explain Spanx, but that's just more consumerism on my part, and she goes right back to looking like a floral sofa (only she's lost weight, so now she's more of a love seat). We're different, my mom and me, and I wouldn't be surprised at all to find out I was switched at birth.

I want her to know that I'm not defective just because I don't think exactly like her. Is that too much to ask? We can have different personalities and still both love Jesus. I fail to see how not being able to make a decoratively crafted fabric apple makes me less of a Christian. Doesn't Jesus need some people who are good with numbers? People who want to be out in the world and live, not just those who want to have a quiet life of crafting? Paul traveled, did he not? Even Jesus traveled!

My mom would say that the gift for numbers is for men—that finance is a "man's job"—but see, that's hard to stomach because I'm tutoring those "men" at school. It's a gift. God just gave it to me. I think he had to notice I was female. He doesn't miss details like that. I mean, the guys at school may not have noticed I'm female, but God knit me together in the womb and all that, so he knows!

Travel journal, you know how extremely strict my parents are, and that would have been fine if they had understood that just because I went to a Christian school, it doesn't mean I was protected from the cruel, harsh world. How much easier my high school life might have been if my parents understood that mean girls are still mean girls, and all the human frailties that still make Lord of the Flies relevant reading go on in every high school across America. Albeit without the pig head. But maybe somewhere in the Midwest where they have access to a pig head, that's part of the deal too. Who knows?

So while guys weren't knocking down my door and I wasn't allowed to date during high school, prom stuck out in my mind as something I had to accomplish. Like a decent SAT score. If I could get to prom, I reasoned that it would make up for my complete lack of a social life during high school. And like I said, through a series of mishaps, I did manage to get there, with Argentine hottie Max Diaz. So I was running the Breathalyzer machine at the front door, but it still counts. Max was a transfer student from Argentina. Sí, el es muy caliente. Very hot! But after graduation, he went back to Buenos Aires to live with his mother and somehow seemed to forget I exist.

Now, I highly doubt that after a nearly perfect record of being dateless throughout high school, anyone is going to remember my brief love connection with the Argentine. Or my brief stint in real jeans. So it's time I wrote off high school altogether and concentrated on my future.

Max wanted to be a preacher, and my parents saw that as the perfect type of husband for me. They allowed a brief "courtship" (emphasis on brief) but then decided I was too young to consider marriage (um, yeah!) and started harping on how difficult a culturally diverse marriage might be. They practically had a parade when he left. In other words, they got scared and decided majoring in finance was better than marrying a foreigner without a real job. Not that he asked for or considered more than a tango at prom, but if that and a full scholarship to Pepperdine make my parents see the benefits of majoring in finance, I'm all for it.

So it's kind of like my life has totally been erased. Everything that happened before now is over, and I get to create a whole new future as a finance major at Pepperdine University in Malibu. Now I can focus on the future and success and what God has for me without being held back by high school.

No one can blame me for feeling defeated at this juncture. I assumed I'd magically wake up, but now I understand that it didn't matter what kind of jeans I wore or even if I wore jeans, since my mother tended to make most of my clothing. But there's a letdown that no one tells you about. You've done it. You've accomplished your goal and graduated with honors and . . . and . . . oh, did we forget to mention that no one cares?

High school graduation is a goal that's given to you. You are not given a choice. You either do the work or you practice this saying: "Would you like fries with that?" After all, we're told, "Go, apply thyself and bring home thy best letter grades so that ye might find a good return in thy labor."

So as a good Christian girl, I did what was commanded of me. I honored my parents—okay, maybe not as well as I could have, but I wore the ugly clothes my mother made. (Look, I know I was lucky to have them and all, but at my wealthy college prep school, homemade clothes are not what you want to stand out for—so go ahead, judge me, but walk a mile in my fake Nikes before you do.) I abstained from makeup and most of the "evils of the vain world," as my mother calls them.

But I did not ever feel that fitting in was evil. God never gave me that mandate. He did, however, tell me to honor my parents. Which I did, but not without a bit of residual effects. I wanted more control. I now see that maybe I could have spent a little of the money I made and done more for myself, but that's another story.

My current story is much more complicated. College begins in two months. I'm on a full-ride scholarship to Pepperdine University to major in finance because I don't ever plan to live hand-to-mouth as my parents seem to. I want more say in my life. More control.

My best friend Claire's father is sending us to Buenos Aires for a graduation trip. That's Argentina! Are you kidding me? Did I hit the jackpot when I chose a best friend or what? I mean, I think my parents might have sprung for a foreign movie festival at the Cineplex, but this!

Buenos Aires . . . sounds like perfection, right? I might see Max. I might learn more about a different culture. I might find they have really great jeans for less down there.

But then the letter came. Once again I had started to fly, and then another weight was added to my wing, pulling me down, down, down to what seems to be my lot in life.

The letter read as follows:

Dear Daisy Crispin:

We look forward to partnering with you, the recipient of this year's Gold Standard Insurance Company scholarship, in a lifetime of good stewardship. As you may have noticed on the list of requirements, Gold Standard asks that all its recipients begin with stewardship of their time. We want all of our students to understand the benefits of stewardship from a human perspective.

Each summer, before tuition and lodging bills are paid, you, Daisy Crispin, will be required to fulfill two full weeks of mission work in the ministry of your choosing. We will count one week already completed in a current mission position, but for at least one week, you must raise your own finances and do such work in another state or, preferably, another country. You may not receive pay for this time, and the forms enclosed will need to be filled out and signed by your immediate superior.

When the forms are received, payment will be remitted to Pepperdine University.

Sincerely,

Bob Torkson

President & CFO
Gold Standard
Insurance Company

All this is well and good, except I'll be in Buenos Aires. Or I won't. I stare at the date. Two months prior! Clearly my letter had taken a vacation of its own, and now I'd pay the price.

My whole world opens up, and I'm not able to enjoy it—I'm allowed to go on an international vacation and see how the "other half" lives, and that other half may end up being the slums of Buenos Aires, not the elite of the South American Paris lounging at the pool.

So it begins, my new travel journal. I'm titling this one "My Life: Stop." Because it's like a bad telegram from my mom's old movies.

"Daisy!" my mom shouts from the house. (My room is in the garage underneath the toilet paper stash in case there's ever a worldwide shortage.)

"Just a minute!" I snap my journal shut, throw a kiss to my David Beckham poster, and slide the journal under my mattress.

"What is it?" I ask as I open the kitchen door.

"Is that any way to ask? Claire's here," Mom says.

Claire's my BFF. She's unfamiliar with the word *no*, and she was not happy about my need to work over the summer versus taking vacation. She feels vacation was my birthright before I submitted to the perils of college so soon after the perils of high school. Yes, I know that's usually the way it goes, but Claire sees the world differently.

Living in Malibu doesn't feel that perilous to me. Nor does a college dorm, where I'll officially not have to share my space with my mother's lifetime supply of toilet paper and craft supplies. My mother runs her own business selling high-end pot holders and aprons to women who shop in fancy cooking stores and never actually cook. The Martha Stewart image is big. Business is good.

But back to my BFF.

Claire's always been a bit of a wild child. She's good at heart, but like a cat, she cannot cure herself of pressing curiosity, even if it leads her into trouble. And it usually does—and takes me right along with her. Then, somehow, I seem to take on the consequences while she skates on with her unusually breezy life. So wrong. Some days I almost feel that's my purpose in life—to take on Claire's consequences—but I'm officially over that job now. She's going to have to find someone else to take the fall.

She looks at me now with her eyebrows knit together. The look that lets me know her discussion is not for my mother's ears.

"We'll be in my room," I say and head out to the garage. Without another word, Claire follows me and shuts the door behind her.

"I've got the answer." She waves a brochure in her hand. "You see, Daisy, you always give up too early. You were just going to nix a free vacation to Argentina—the land of the tango, the land of Max Diaz. But I, your best friend, persevere. I'm like that, you know."

I roll my eyes. "Except when it comes to homework."

"International ministry exchange." She waves the brochure again.

"Pardon?"

"I found a ministry online where you trade with someone, go to their country, and learn the needs, and they come here." Claire pauses. "By that, I mean they come to my house, because I'm not sure yours exactly represents America as people imagine it." She scrunches her nose as she looks around my garage/room.

"I think I'm offended."

"No you're not." Claire breezes past me and makes sure my door is firmly shut. "You see your reality, even if you want to make me the bad guy for pointing it out. It's hard to explain your house to a foreigner. It's hard to explain your house to anyone."

I feel the need to defend my mother. "True, but my mom would be great with a foreign missionary. Let me see that." I reach for the brochure.

Claire pulls it away. "Wait a minute. This is my idea."

"My mom would show them how to make the most of living in a wealthy place with few resources. That's a skill anyone but you could learn and use."

"If the missionary could find her in this mess, sure. But Daisy, you've got your grandparents' furniture in the living room while they remodel, your mother's craft supplies everywhere while she expands the business, and then there's your father's costumes. Seriously, I've known you practically your whole life and it's never been this bad. How would you explain that to someone in a foreign language? *Este es hoarders, no?*"

"Not funny. Don't they expect to go into a Christian home? Christians usually live frugally," I say, trying delicately to avoid calling her parents heathens, or young in their faith.

"You're getting lost in the minut-ay."

"Minutia."

"I graduated high school. You're done correcting me. If it's wrong, change the dictionary." Claire sulks. "New words are created every day. It's strategery."

I stare at the brochure in her hand. A woman in a colorful dress is posed for the tango. "I do so want to go to Argentina. Just when I think it's safe to embrace something good, another stick gets thrown into my wheel spoke."

"Only if you let it. Your problem is when someone tells you no, you're too quick to believe it."

"Because I have no other choice," I tell her. "Besides, I would think it's part of the requirement that a visiting missionary stay with a Christian family."

"My family is Christian, Daisy. Maybe not the same way yours is, but my mom could certainly make sure they get to church, and they'd have my car to drive while they were here. They could just work in the food bank at church like you do."

"You know what my mom will say. I can just stay and work at the food bank."

"I can't believe your mother would let you turn down a free trip to Argentina over a few details."

"I'm only saying if you're planning to trade with a Christian ministry, my parents seem to have the obvious home for them. Not your mansion in the hills."

"Like they'd complain! Maybe they'd learn that they want to go to college and sponsor a church back home or the like." Claire lies down on my bed. She's wearing a black maxi dress to her ankles with big, clunky red shoes, costume jewelry up her arm—nearly to her shoulder—and a long, genuine strand of pearls. In other words, a typical afternoon outfit for Claire.

Claire's father is a well-known attorney. My dad's an actor. A self-employed actor, which means he does a lot of singing telegrams dressed as fowl, crustaceans, and *Star Trek* characters. You wouldn't think there was a huge market for that kind of thing, but apparently the engineers of Silicon Valley like to say it in song. It helps that my father speaks Romulan.

Mom makes Dad's costumes and now has her own line of upscale novelty aprons and oven mitts. This year it officially became a business —and it cracks me up that my mother would never pay for store-bought jeans, but she has the gall to sell overpriced kitchenware in that same mall I felt banned from.

Now, my parents love Jesus, and they are the salt of the earth, but if you came to our house on any given day, you'd definitely think they were your ministry. Or that *Hoarders* had missed a house, as Claire implied. I want to defend my parents, but truthfully, I don't have a lot of ground to stand on here—it's covered with fabric, furniture, and household supplies.

I stare at the vat of pickles on a nearby shelf perched over my bed. "Yes, definitely your house," I agree as I take a more realistic, detached look at reality. "Let me see what it says." I grab the brochure and see pictures of adorable, olive-skinned children without shoes, in tattered pants, and I hear the Spanish plea for "May I have some more, sir?" in my head. "It's positively Dickensian."

"I know, right? But with a Latino flair." Claire wiggles her eyebrows. "And I'm sure some young, unattached polo players tango as well." She sits up on my bed. "But we won't tell your parents that part. I'm telling you, put in the time—you can do one week in Argentina—then we relax for the next week and soak in the sun and the sights."

"You really do think outside the box."

"Someone has to. The mission person signs off on your paperwork, and then we head to the spa and learn to tango. What could be more beautiful?"

"It sounds too simple. There has to be a catch. There's always a catch. This is me we're talking about."

"Quit being so paranoid. Call the number and get it arranged. They call your pastor, your scholarship program, and we are in business and get the pampering vacation we deserve after surviving St. James College Prep. Plus it helps your parents know we're not just going to Argentina to get into trouble or to see Max."

"I have to Skype Max," I say with a flutter in my stomach, finally allowing myself to believe I'll be in Max Diaz's homeland. It felt too huge to hope for. "I can't believe I'll be in his hometown! Buenos Aires, land of the tango, the South American Paris . . ."

"The fine South American leather collection!"

I start to get excited and can feel my heart getting all aflutter too. "This might really happen."

"Max is going to freak. I'll bet you he never thought this would happen, with your parents." Claire blows on her fingernails, which she has just finished painting.

"Freak in a good way? Or in a bad, 'I'm seriously stalking him' way?"

"A good way!"

My immediate reaction is fear. "I'll freak him out. He'll think I want a proposal."

"He knows you're going to college in August at Pepperdine. He knows this is nothing more than a sweet, summer romance of the G-rated kind."

I raise my eyebrows.

"Okay, PG. You can kiss him, but nothing more, or your parents will have my head."

"Deal," I tell her with a handshake. "Max is my first love, my boyfriend." I allow myself that thought. I know I'm young and all (eighteen in three months), but I'm a romantic, and even though Max had to go back home to Argentina, I never quite believed it would be the last of him. Maybe because my parents got married in college. I know it's ridiculous, but what kind of romantic would I be if I didn't allow myself to dream?

"Oh, it's going to happen. It's time you learned the power of positive thinking, Daisy. We are going to Buenos Aires, the most cosmopolitan city of South America, and even better? We'll know someone there who can show us the ropes!"

I clutch the brochure to my heart. "It is. It is going to happen."

I ignore that nagging kernel of truth in my soul. The one

that tells me nothing ever goes as planned with Claire. The one that asks me, where is the history that dictates a successful future here? The one that tells me maybe planning a ministry with the express plan to get to an international spa is not what my scholarship provider hoped to accomplish by sending me on a mission.

But I ignore all those ugly truths because baby, I am going to Buenos Aires! Swimming pools, the tango, and the icing on the Latino cake: Max Diaz in his native surroundings.

2

My mom, as I expected, is much less enthusiastic about the idea. She's folding fabric on the dinner table so that we can find a spot to eat. "How do you expect to have an effective ministry in a country you know nothing about, in a language you barely speak?"

"That's what the exchange program is all about. Mom, you're always telling me how those Bible translator friends of yours go into foreign countries where they don't know a word of the tribe's language. Surely this will be easier for me with my Spanish and Latin classes."

She looks at the neat pile of patriotic fabric. "I don't know. Claire and you in a foreign country?"

"You have to trust me at some point, Mom. I'll be on my own in two months. You could make some blankets, and I could take them with me. That would be a nice entry into the mission."

"Doesn't this stuff have to be prearranged a long time in advance?"

"Yes, but Claire's father offered to make a donation in exchange for expediency. He's already booked our flights and he doesn't want to rebook them."

"He shouldn't have done that without asking us first."

"Mom!" I whine. I shake the letter in my hand. "It's all right with the scholarship fund. If they can trust me, can't you?"

My dad walks into the kitchen.

"Dad," I say in my most adult voice.

He turns back around when he sees my mom and me looking at him. He waves a hand. "Not getting involved."

"Dear!" my mom says in that voice that makes Dad do an about-face. "Your daughter wants to go to Argentina on a mission trip, not just stay in that nice hotel Claire's parents booked."

"Oh," my dad says, rubbing his head. "Is that safe?"

"No!" my mom says.

"It's safe, and then I'll get to see the real Argentina, not just the tourist traps. Please, Dad! It's the only way I'm going to complete the mission work in time for school and still get my graduation trip with Claire."

"But two young girls alone in a foreign country outside of the hotel? It's a recipe for trouble. You see that all the time on the news. And those are only the ones we hear about," Mom says.

"I want to have a great adventure. Gil told me that once the work starts, there never seems to be time for adventure. If not now, when?"

"When you're not my responsibility," Dad says.

"I don't know," Mom says. "Chasing a boy halfway around the world? Do you think that's the sort of girl the future Pastor Max would want to marry?"

I exhale loudly. "I'm not going to Argentina for Max." *He's just part of the excursion package.* "And I'm certainly not marrying anyone until I'm done with college."

"I said that once," my mother says dreamily, staring at my father.

"Ew. Things are different now, Mom. I need college, and I especially need it for finance."

"We were young once too," Dad says.

"No, you never were. Mom was born eighty. And I don't even know if I'll see Max. Of course I'll try, I'm not going to lie. He might never come back to the States again, and it's not like I've lost any admiration for him. I just know where my priorities are. He knows his."

"That's what all young people say before their hormones do the talking for them."

"Ew, Dad. Must you always take it to the hormonal level? Gross."

"What does Claire's father say about this? Does he know that Claire will be on her own at the hotel while you're working with this mission?"

"Obviously, he's paying for it, so he must trust us."

"He trusts you because he doesn't know half of what his daughter does."

"Well, that's true."

Dad sighs heavily. "I'm sure he thought we'd never let you go. That's probably why he felt safe saying yes to Claire. I'd like to call him and see if he knows Claire will be alone at the hotel while you're doing this ministry. They seem to rely on you to keep an eye on her."

My mom lifts the brochure from my hands. "Hands of Love!" she says.

I nod. "That's the name of the ministry."

"It can't be. Honey, look," she says to my father, handing him the brochure.

"Maybe it's God's will," my father says. He looks at my mother as if something miraculous has taken place.

"What are the chances?" Mom asks.

"God's world is smaller than we imagine."

"What are you both talking about?" I ask. Implied: *And will it benefit me?*

"This ministry. Hands of Love." My dad shakes the brochure. "It's run by your mother's college roommate. I'll be, it's a small world, isn't it?"

"It's not!" I shout, hoping against hope that what they said isn't true. Because for all intents and purposes, I do want to see Max, and if I have another mom checking on me every five minutes, that's not going to happen. "Maybe it's just someone with the same name," I suggest. "It's probably a common name, right, Mom?"

"Not all that common. It's her. We talked about her being down there when you and Claire first came up with this trip. I thought we might look her up back then, remember, dear?"

Dad nods.

"Her name is Libby Bramer. I can't imagine there are two of them in Buenos Aires. I wonder if she recognized your name, or haven't you applied yet? Either way, I'll feel so much better if Libby is running the ministry."

I plead the fifth here. "So she didn't ever get married? Or that's her married name?"

"Hmm," my dad says. "I doubt she got married."

"Honey!" my mom says.

"She was . . . let me think about how to say this kindly . . . she was kind of a man-hater," my father says.

"That's your kindler, gentler answer?" Mom asks.

"In a word, yes. She paid a lot of attention to what others

did back in the day. Liked to run the show, if you will. We tended to avoid her if at all possible."

Great.

"*You* tended to avoid her," Mom says. "She's lovely, Daisy. She's very independent, and you would like that."

"I'm sure I will. Besides, how much trouble could I get into with a man-hating missionary who knows my parents?"

"Daisy! Libby is not a man-hater! Besides, even if she was, that was a long time ago. People change, and I'm sure she's matured," Mom says. My father is behind her shaking his head, but he begins nodding when she turns to face him.

"Libby doesn't give me all that much peace of mind, actually. And your father did say we could use his airline miles," Dad says to Mom. "That's one way we could make this happen."

"That's not necessary. Claire's dad is buying the tickets with his miles. It's all set up. My passport should be here any day."

"For us," Mom says to me. "I think your father is talking about us. We're not sending our daughter to a foreign country alone to work in missions. Not without us."

My lungs empty. "You don't trust me at all. I'll be living on my own in two months. How can you not trust me? What difference does it make now?"

"Two months, a few thousand miles, and a foreign language. Quite a bit of difference. I don't want to hear you've been picked up in some foreign gutter," Mom says. "We trust you, Daisy. It's your ability to adjust to a different world we don't trust. You've lived a very sheltered life."

"Because you've created that sheltered life!"

"Quit acting so innocent. You and Claire have something

up your sleeve. I'm sure it has something to do with Max," Dad says. "This conversation is over. If you choose to do your mission work in Argentina, we're going with you. It's that simple. Or you have another option: you can continue to work at the food bank this summer and declare hardship as your reason for not completing the stipulations."

"This has nothing to do with Max," I argue. "I mean, sure, I want to see him, but my decision is separate from that. I'll admit, Claire and I planned our destination because we wanted to do something more exotic than the standard Hawaii, but I assure you, my decision has nothing to do with that now. But we thought with Max there, we'd have some connection to the country if we got into trouble. It's actually very responsible."

"Uh-huh."

"Mom, you've never been out of the country. Don't you regret that? Do you want me to have the same regrets? Never having the chance to travel?" I flutter my lashes to reiterate my innocent desires.

"I don't care for travel. It's always so hard to get sewing supplies and figure out what your father will eat. I just never cared for all of the unknowns, but if this means that much to you, maybe it's time I made an exception. I wonder how long it will take us to get our passports."

"No, not you, Mom. Me. I totally understand that you don't want to travel, I get it. It's a total hassle. I'm only saying that *I* want to travel. I want to see the world and find out what makes people tick, and I can't do that here."

"Daisy, people from all over the world live right here in Silicon Valley. You can absolutely do that here. What about the food bank? You've given so much time to them already.

You don't think Pastor will be offended that you're spending your ministry time in another country?"

"Pastor would want to see me try new things. How do I know that the food bank is where I want to spend my time when there might be a better use of my skills elsewhere?"

"I think he might say you could use your skills elsewhere here, but maybe that's me," Dad says.

My desperation is growing as I feel that much closer to actually getting out of this country and seeing the world. Without my parents. For once I'd be free of the chains that bind me to my lack of options and responsibilities. "I want to stretch my wings! I'm tired of doing exactly as I'm told. Maybe I'm meant for more than this provincial life!" I say, quoting my favorite Disney princess.

"Maybe you're not," Mom says. "Look, if you want to go to Buenos Aires, Dad and I are willing to entertain the notion, but only if we come with you. There's a news story on every night that tells of some young girls disappearing."

"That's why you shouldn't watch the news. It makes you feel like the world is made up of nothing but sociopaths and junkies."

"Do you want me to ask Grandpa for his miles or don't you? You've been given your choice."

I sigh. "Fine."

"Great!" Mom claps her hands together. "I'll call Libby and get the mission set up and ensure all the paperwork is done from her side. That way we'll know when we need to travel. What day do you have to be at school, Daisy?"

"August twenty-third." I sigh. "I'm going to email Claire." Who, I might add, is going to kill me. Our freewheeling, luxury spa vacation has just turned into a working nightmare in a flea-ridden barrio with chaperones. Not just chaperones, but my parents, which will be like inviting Mother Teresa to the spa: guilt-inducing and not all that fun.

I'm beginning to think life is all about lowering my expectations.

My Life: Stop—July 6

Fun travel factoid: Argentina comes from the Latin Argentum, translated "land of silver." Or, in my case, "land of silver bars." Because let's face it, my parents will never let me out.

I thought this airplane ride would be my flight into freedom—off we go into the wild blue yonder and all that—but as I watch my mom and dad joke with the flight attendants, it's more like a jail bus. The next stop is hard labor camp, complete with the chain around my leg.

Why is it that adults want you to learn everything through pain and suffering? Is it me? Whatever happened to the world of Barney and learning through fun, purple dinosaurs?

I've read all of my magazines, a few of Claire's (the secular ones my mom says are of the devil), and started a book. But I can't concentrate. In less than an hour, I will be on foreign ground. Land of Max Diaz, polo, and empire penguins. My version of milk and honey. A place where no one knows I wore homemade clothes or was perfectly dateless. This might be the beginning of *the whole new me, and I might come home with a new confidence. My perspective could change and my future could open up. Even my parents being along can't stop my excitement from forming now. My world is about to expand. Mas grande.*

The plane comes to a smooth landing, almost as though we've gracefully entered the country on ballet toes. "We're here!"

Claire grabs my hands. "We made it!" Her smile is contagious, and we both start to giggle as if we pulled off some great crime.

"Let's go," my father orders. "We have to grab our bags and get to the hotel, and to Libby's by dark. Move!"

The airport is cavernous, loud, and crowded, but nothing can hide my fervor as I read every luxurious advertisement and try to translate it with my poor Spanish skills. "*Hola!*" I say to everyone as we pass by. "*Hola! Como está?*" I say to complete strangers as we rush by them in my father's hurry to get to the baggage claim before anyone else.

When we arrive at the luggage carousel, it's spinning with no sign of our bags—or anyone's, for that matter. "It looks like we beat the luggage. Why don't you get the bags, girls, and meet us outside while we flag a cab?"

"Pierce," my mom says. "We have time. Do you really want to leave the girls here alone already? Besides, isn't there customs?"

My dad visibly calms. "Right. We can wait, I suppose."

I stop and spin in the center of the domed, hangar-like building. "Wow," I say, staring up at the roof. "I feel different here. Like I've suddenly grown up. I can't wait to have my first Argentine steak. That will make it official."

Claire grabs my hand again. "Would you come on? This isn't a musical. You're going to get robbed if you keep looking like the typical tourist."

"But it is a musical to me because I'm hearing echoes of a hot Latino singer in my ears. His passionate voice tells me he wants to be my hero, and standing here in Buenos Aires, I can't help but believe it." I belt out my song. "He could kiss away my tears!"

Claire stops me and grabs me by the shoulders. "Daisy, I'm going to tell you this once, and you're going to hear it. Ever since you first laid eyes on Chase in kindergarten, you've had this runaway romantic imagination."

"You're sucking out the fun from this trip and we haven't even left the airport."

Claire pushes her dark hair over her ear. "Far be it from me to kill a dream, but Chase turned out to be a tool and it took you way too long to believe it."

"No, you're totally right. Chase is a nub. I should have seen it when he first liked Amber."

Claire yawns, but she keeps her focus on me intently. "Max left California, so I want that reality to settle in, all right? He may be a really nice guy, but the chance of something happening between you two, with an ocean and a bajillion countries in between you, is slim at best."

"I won't get hurt," I tell Claire. "I just want to have a romantic goodbye, is that too much to ask?"

"Promise me you're not going to make more of this trip or of him than is actually there. Even if Max sweeps you off your feet, you're going to college in a month and a half, and this is nothing more than a mild, albeit international, flirtation."

"But—"

"Promise."

"What's going on back there?" My dad turns toward us. "Pick up your luggage, let's get on with this."

"Nothing!" I loosen myself from Claire's grip. "Come on, we have to go!" We stand by my father as we await the luggage to rescue it from its ride. Next, we look forward to the invasion of privacy that is customs. At least, that's the way Claire has explained it. She told me we'd get electronically assaulted with the X-ray machines of security in America and then we'd get the hand version on our property in Argentina.

Claire grabs my elbow. "Just tell me you're not imagining some wild *Notebook* kind of reunion."

"Of course not," I say, but bite down on my bottom lip. I mean, really, what would be wrong with that? Doesn't Claire have a romantic bone in her body?

"I knew it!" Claire yells. "I can see it in your eyes. Get out of your dream world! How can you be so good at math and then have this wild imagination? The two don't go together. Daisy, guys our age are not thinking about forever. You're only going to get hurt, and I don't want to nurse you back to health in a foreign country. I'm here to relax and enjoy the luxuries of Latino food, good shopping, and a spa where I can't understand a word the aesthetician says, so there is no reason to be polite. Hence, more relaxation."

"Finance majors need love too," I say. "Can't I be good at math and have a romantic life?"

Claire sighs her annoyance. "You are so warped. I'm going to have to deal with the fallout when reality doesn't live up to your romantic expectations, so I'm asking you nicely—dwell with the rest of us in the real world. Max was a dance, that's all." Claire shakes her head slowly. "He is not going to come to your rescue, he is not going to be riding a white horse, and he is not going to change his mind about living in his home country for this movie ending you're dreaming up. All right?"

My dad is pointing at his watch, so what else can I do but agree? "All right."

"And I know what you're thinking, so get it out of your mind!"

The truth is, it doesn't quite leave my mind. Not as we gather our luggage, not as we wait in several lines.

I sigh as we wait for the inefficiency that is customs. From the tall ceiling hang flag advertisements for luxury goods. "There are benefits to making new friends," I tell Claire.

"Real friends tell you the truth. Real friends don't want you to prolong the suffering if there's going to be suffering."

"There's not going to be suffering!"

"Would you girls hustle it along?" my dad snaps. "You can talk in the taxi."

There are pictures of the city lining the airport walkway, and I'm shocked at how much like San Francisco it appears. Beautiful architecture, water everywhere, and from the sounds of it, lots of people speaking loudly. It's like I'm in North Beach. The brochure did say that Buenos Aires had a large population of Italians.

The airport is bustling, and there's so much going on around me, I'm on high alert, ready to be knocked over the head. I'm almost happy my parents came with us. Almost.

"Did you hide your money all over your body, like I told you?" Claire asks as we wait on the curb outside the bustling airport. There are funky little cars that look like PT Cruisers along the walkway, and across the street is a forest of tropical trees that I've never seen before. The air feels cold and heavy with moisture. There are so many conversations going on around me in Spanish, I can't separate one of them to hear what's being said.

Claire speaks again. "Well, did you hide your money?"

"What? Yeah. I'm a walking piggy bank," I tell her. "Look at those trees. What do you think they are?"

"I don't care. I just want to get to the hotel and sleep. My father told me that we're not supposed to talk to anyone. They can all be charming, sort of like your Max. We're not supposed to be charmed by chivalry. We're just supposed to get to the hotel without speaking to anyone if possible."

"We live in Silicon Valley. With Spock personalities by the thousands. How is it we're not to be moved by chivalry and manners?"

"My father just said not to talk to anyone we don't know," Claire says.

"You told me that on the plane. Forty times. Since when are you the safety monitor? Are you nervous?" I glance at my parents. "Do you think my parents would let us talk to someone we don't know? Much less a handsome Argentine with manners?" I laugh. "Besides, we barely speak Spanish. What are we going to say—'where is the bathroom?' *Dónde está el baño?* And wait to be swept off our feet?"

"My father has traveled all over the world, Daisy, and he said to act authoritative and not like we're tourists. That makes us a target."

"You are nervous! I can hardly believe it. The girl who once tried to wear a spider nose ring to a Christian school is nervous." I grin. Somehow it makes me feel strangely powerful to watch Claire act nervous. As long as I've known her, she's always been the first one in—the girl who would enter the lion's den with confidence.

"I'm only trying to help you," Claire says. "You haven't traveled a lot."

"Or at all, but face it, we have 'tourist' written all over us. My dad is wearing a Hawaiian shirt and sandals with socks. My mom has on a muumuu. We're not exactly stealth. If you looked in an encyclopedia under 'tourist,' my parents' picture would be there."

My dad is engaged in some sort of negotiations with the cab driver amid all the chaos of the airport, which seems small now that we're outside. Claire's eyes are shifting all over, taking in as much of her surroundings as she can. Honestly, she makes my parents look sophisticated at the moment, and for once in her life she seems uncomfortable in her element.

Wonders never cease. Claire is more afraid of this trip than I am.

3

Personal space is going to be an issue for me in Argentina, I can tell already. People talk loud. They talk close. When it was hottie Max talking closely and those deep brown eyes staring down at me, ask me if I cared how loudly he talked. Now insert an old taxi driver with breath that could choke a horse, and I have an issue. I'm trying to translate for my father, but it is not going well, and I'm in desperate need of oxygen. Between the cabbie's breath and the cigarette smoke in the air . . .

"Señor Crispin! Mr. Crispin!"

I think I'm imagining it. I check frantically around me.

"Max? Claire, did you hear Max?" I ask her.

She shakes her head and rolls her eyes. "Didn't I talk to you about this?"

Then I hear it again and this time I know it's not my imagination.

"Señor Crispin!" Max's voice breaks over the noise, and like a beautiful, perfect note, it rises over the chaos and attracts my attention with laser-beam precision.

"Max! I knew it was him!" I tap my dad on the shoulder. "Dad, it's Max!" I point. Is it possible he grew more handsome since I saw him last? I mean, not that I'm shallow and that's what I care about, but it sure doesn't hurt that he's straight out of a telenovela.

Max smiles and waves at me from the huge white van he's driving. I think my heart stops for a minute as I take in the sight of him. His smile could melt the coldest of hearts.

"He's cuter in his natural habitat," Claire states.

"Is that even possible?" I ask. "Hey, he's not a zoo animal."

"So you're saying I can't throw him a piece of meat? He won't do a trick?"

"His outside is gorgeous, but it's the soft, gooey soul that I love." I let out a dreamy sigh. "Hi, Max! Hi!"

"There is something seriously wrong with you. What's he doing here? He knows we're here on vacation and your ministry, right? He doesn't expect to be spending time with you. My dad paid for the trip, you know. It's supposed to be girl time."

"We can all be friends. You sound like when we were in grade school and you wouldn't let me be friends with Lacey Buckout."

"I planned for us to lounge around like slugs, and now you're working half the time we're here. Can you blame me that I don't want all that other half spent with Antonio Banderas and his big Puss in Boots eyes?"

"It looks like he's picking us up!" I squeal. "I told him when we were arriving, but he thought he'd be working." I try to keep the giddy out of my voice, but let's face it, I'm giddy.

My dad wastes no time in picking up the bags and heading over to the utilitarian white van (the favorite of child molesters everywhere). Max hops out, opens the double back doors, and helps my dad lift in the suitcases. He's wearing jeans with holes in the legs and a collared, button-up shirt that's neither buttoned-up nor stuffy.

"Get in." Max drops the first bag and my smile falters. He notices my expression and comes straight over to me. "Welcome. *Bienvenidos, señorita.*" He leans in and kisses my cheek like I'm a nun, then looks back at my father, but Dad is so involved with luggage he doesn't have time to notice a thing. Which makes the moment more blissful than ever—until I catch my mom's evil eye.

"It's cultural," I say as I slide past her into the van. "Doesn't the Bible say to greet each other with a holy kiss? Can't get much holier than that."

I realize it's true as I watch him give the same kiss to Claire. Max doesn't like me. Not in the way he did, anyway. I run through the memories in my head and try to think why he doesn't like me in that way, but looking around at the new-fangled trees and the colors of Argentina, I don't care that much. I wasted so many years analyzing Chase. If he noticed what I wore that day. If he liked my hair. If his locker was next to mine. And what did it get me but heartache?

If I've learned any lesson in my years of being pathetic and dateless, it's that fawning over a guy who doesn't want me is wasted energy. Someday some younger version of my nerdy father will come along and sweep me into his crumpled Hyundai and I'll forget the tango or Chase's pyro tendencies ever existed.

But I still have to mourn the loss. I just don't want to lose my vacation doing so, so I'm going to write in my travel journal. That way I can write all those sad feelings down and feel them later rather than now—when there is Argentine steak to be eaten and Vacation Bible School to plan.

I will not spend my first foreign vacation mourning something that evidently existed only in my head.

Max squeezes my hand, and I question romance again! He jogs around to the side of the van to help the ladies inside, and I'm enamored at how, like Zorro, Max comes at exactly the right time. We just don't see enough of that anymore. I'm not a big believer in my hero arriving on a white horse, but I'm not completely against the idea either. Let's face it, it doesn't hurt that he looks like an Argentine polo player.

My mom climbs into the van with Claire while my father gets into the passenger seat—which leaves me in the backseat, the farthest possible place from Max. Within seconds we're on our way, and Max peels out of the airport.

"I cannot wait to show you around, but I think today is going to be my limit," he says. "My mom has a busy agenda for me before classes start."

"Looking for excuses?" Claire asks.

"Huh?"

"Nothing."

I look for a way to break the tension. "We're staying at the Palace Alvear. Well, I'm staying there later, after the mission trip. Claire's there now, so you can drop us off."

Max whistles. "Wow, really? By yourself?" He turns and looks at Claire.

She lifts one side of her mouth in a taunting smile. "Yes. It's one of the safest areas. In Recoleta, near the cemetery. My parents researched thoroughly before they booked."

"I know where it is, Claire, but I wouldn't go out alone. You don't speak Spanish well enough, and I'd advise the same thing if you were in San Francisco. You sort of tend to find trouble. No offense."

"None taken," Claire says with tightened lips.

"What will you do until Daisy gets back from her missionary work?"

"I'll keep busy." Claire swallows visibly. "Well, I thought Daisy's parents were staying with me, but they booked elsewhere. There's room," she says to my parents.

"After seeing the prices, I assumed they booked elsewhere." Max laughs, but Claire's eyes are round like DVDs. It unnerves me to see her nervous. I didn't know she had it in her.

"I assume the concierge can set me up on tours where I'll be perfectly safe." There's still a question mark in her tone.

"Naturally. Just check with the concierge. I'm sure it will be fine." He turns around and stares ominously.

Claire's tone changes and grows attitude. "You know, this was supposed to be a luxury vacation, but then Sarika and Angie pulled out, saying their parents wouldn't let them go, and then Daisy has to do this mission thing, and everything got all messed up. I had it all planned that we'd be together in a group. Now you're telling me I'll be stuck in some luxury hotel alone and literally in a gilded cage?"

"No," Max says. "I didn't mean that, and I'm sure you'll be safe with the concierge guiding you. If you want, I'm sure I can find friends who would be happy to take you around."

I feel guilty now. Guilty for going on a mission trip. Only I would run into trouble for going on a mission trip instead of staying in a luxurious hotel. Something is wrong here.

Suddenly the whole van becomes quiet and it's beyond awkward. I lean forward on the seat and rest my chin between my mom and Claire.

"I'm sorry, Claire," I tell her. "I should have just canceled. I couldn't jeopardize my scholarship for a vacation."

"No, I know. It sucks being poor. I get it."

My mom and dad both turn to look at her, and she realizes her mistake immediately. "I didn't mean—oh, never mind. I'm just tired. Let's get to the hotel and forget I said that."

"Claire," my mother interjects calmly. "That hotel price per night is higher than our family mortgage. I understand your parents want you to have this celebration and they've given you an incredible gift, but as Daisy's parents—remember she's still not eighteen until September—we felt it was a bit dangerous for two young girls, yet we didn't want her to miss the experience. Then there was the scholarship requirement to deal with. It just worked out this way. I know it's always been hard for you two to have such different upbringings, but our hope was that you'd learn from each other."

"No, it's fine. I'm just disappointed, is all, and tired from the trip. Let's forget I said anything."

Max turns around and smiles with a warmth I feel in my stomach. "Daisy always has put others before herself. It's one of the things I love best about her."

Did he just say *love*? He loves something about me?

Claire stares a hole in my face, willing me not to read too much into the comment, and I feel the need to defend her. "You're not selfish," I tell her. "You planned a fabulous vacation, and I'm only sorry I can't fully experience it with you." What I'm really sorry about is that her parents didn't ever think to come, or think of her safety in a foreign country, other than the standard blurb from a travel brochure. It breaks my heart, and I feel strangely protective of her. "We're going to have a great time. I won't be at the mission the whole time. I'll concentrate on the work, get it done, and be back before you know it. Then you can show me around Recoleta."

A single tear falls from Claire's eyes. "No, I know. Let's just go to the hotel. I'm tired, that's all."

I feel terrible. Claire's life is so lonely, and never is it more apparent to me how much she's had to be on her own until this moment. I'm sick over the fact that she's virtually raised herself or been at my sorry little house instead of her mansion for most of her days. I don't say anything more to her for fear she'll break into full-blown tears.

"Max, will I meet your mother while we're here?" I ask.

"Oh," he stammers. "Did you want to?"

"Not if it's inconvenient, but you know, I loved your father so much that I thought I'd like to see the other half of your parents."

"I'd like to meet her too," Mom says. "See how much we have in common parenting across the globe."

Max twists his head toward my mother so fast it's like something out of a horror film. "My mother? No, she's . . . she likes to stay in the house. But I have so much to show you, we'll hardly have time to go by my house."

Mom misses the clues. "I'd love to meet her. Maybe we can take her out to dinner."

"Probably not. She's not really social in that way. The rest of Buenos Aires is, so you'll have no trouble finding friends for dinner. My mom doesn't like to leave the house much."

"My wife has no trouble finding friends anywhere, Max. She just wants to meet your mother," Dad says. "Maybe we could bring her dinner. We wouldn't want to intrude."

"Yeah, sure," Max says without committing. *He can't commit to a dinner?* Suddenly Max is a whole lot less attractive to me. I mean, we did head around the globe to see him. Is dinner really that out of the ordinary? In a Latino country known for its hospitality?

The drive to the center of town is gorgeous. The water is murky gray, matching the overcast sky, but the city is bright, like an old provincial city in Europe. The people are beautiful. And thin.

As we arrive at the hotel, it doesn't escape me that I've brought my own entourage of drama, and maybe I've over-extended myself just a bit coming on this trip. Maybe I should have stayed home and gotten ready for college by visiting Staples and working at the food bank I already know. Why do I have to mess up on such a spectacular level? And at such great expense?

A guy in a uniform that looks like he should be guarding a queen somewhere opens the van's door. He rambles a welcome in Spanish and switches to English when he takes one look at my father.

"Welcome. Checking in with us today?"

"No, just dropping off our girl here. Don't need any help, thank you," my dad says with a wave.

Translation: *I'm not tipping.* The message is received because the bellman scurries off.

"I'm checking in with you, Claire, because there's no need for anyone to know you're here alone," Dad says. "Daisy, you come with me so it doesn't look improper." He looks at Max. "You in a hurry, son? We can take a taxi over to the mission if you are."

"I wouldn't hear of it," Max says. "I'll just park over there near the exit, and you come out when you're ready."

"So is it me?" I whisper to Claire. "Why does Max seem

so secretive, and why doesn't he just leave if he doesn't want to introduce me to his mom?"

Claire looks back. "He's a freak and he's not worthy of you."

"Why don't you tell me how you really feel?"

"Look, you always pick these hot-and-cold types, and they're freaks. You need someone who is constant. Even if he's constantly a jerk, at least you know who he is. The last thing anyone needs is a moody boyfriend. He's a mama's boy." Claire hikes her handbag over her shoulder. "If you're not good enough for his mama, you're too good for him, in my opinion."

I want to stay with Max if only to prove Claire isn't right about him, but with a sick feeling in the pit of my stomach, I suddenly wonder. Maybe I'm not a good judge of character like I've always thought. Maybe my romantic pixie dust gets in the way of my vision of reality.

One look from Claire and I head into the hotel. I shoot Max a look of sorrow and he blows me a kiss.

What it means, I'll never know.

4

Walking into the magnificent hotel and its expansive foyer makes me realize how shallow I am. I've spent my entire school career being shown things Claire's gotten that are new and incredible, and they're always more than I hope to obtain in this lifetime. But I know they don't really satisfy. I read it in the Bible. I see it in Claire's eyes. And yet my mind always goes back to what I don't have. Sometimes I hate my humanity.

I think that was why I got interested in finance in the first place. Not necessarily because of what money could buy, but for the order and the freedom from chaos that seemed to be in every luxurious spot Claire ever took me. Cleanliness and expansiveness—it made me feel alive and want to dance. Rich people have places to store their toilet paper, and with their four-plus bathrooms, even the Costco megapack finds a home. Having always felt like the world was closing in on me, I admired this.

How I envied Claire for not having to announce to the world that her family used toilet paper. It was done quietly. Discreetly. There's something so elegant in that. And let's not even get started on the fact that rich people have guest bathrooms, which means no one is going in there to open the medicine cabinet and find your father's Preparation H tumbling down. Of course, maybe their guests don't open the medicine cabinet to begin with.

There's beauty in order. In having a place for everything. Oh, the freedom that comes from having extra.

Claire steps up to the desk.

"I wonder if they'll have the toilet paper in a little triangle," I say. "You think?"

Claire sighs. "You're impressed by that? They do that at Motel 6."

This takes the wind out of my sails. "Well, I would like it. Someone took the time to fold the little toilet paper ending. I think that's sweet."

Claire scoffs at this and turns back to the desk manager. "Checking in. Claire Webber." She hands over her credit card as if she's been doing this for years.

I realize she seems like a total brat, but my best friend really just overcompensates when she's scared. And isn't a best friend someone who loves you despite your faults? I mean, she put up with my bad clothes, my lack of makeup, and my hectic work schedule. Not only that, she'd spend the night at my house amid the rolls of excess toilet paper when she could have been home in crisp, clean, *Architectural Digest*–style beauty. Instead, she ate my mom's meatloaf and slept under towers of TP. Friendship is a beautiful thing.

The man hands Claire her card back, welcomes her with a list of services available at the hotel, and sends her on to the gold elevators. My father never says a word. I hate to see him struggle in this fancy hotel, but I know he does. It's written all over his face.

The gold elevator doors open and close. The bellman who wrestled my father for Claire's luggage pushes the button and says nothing until the doors open again. He extends his arm and motions for us to exit, then he follows us with Claire's bags. He leads us to a double door, unlocks it, and pushes it open into a cavernous room with faux marble columns and old European-style decorating. There's red and gold plush carpeting, deep French chairs covered in red tapestry, and a gold and crystal chandelier centered over the Queen Anne mahogany bed. Draperies of gold plunge into a puddle on the floor, and Claire and I run to the window.

"That's the famous Recoleta cemetery," the bellman says. "One of the best views of the city. Eva Perón is buried there, and it's one of the main tourist attractions."

"Who?" Claire asks.

"'Don't cry for me, Argentina'!" I wail, and her theater background kicks in immediately.

"Oh, right."

I'm stunned at the view, both in and out of the suite. It's like nothing I've ever seen, and it makes me want to dance to classical music. "This room is fit for seventeenth-century royalty."

"No, no, no," the bellman says. "This is for modern royalty. We have a full spa downstairs, two restaurants, and room service, of course, and all the modern-day conveniences for your television viewing and your computer. Your butler will be in to show you around and unpack your items within the half hour. In the meantime, is there anything I can get for you?"

"A butler?" Claire asks.

"Your parents from America? They have requested a butler for you while your friend stays elsewhere."

"Oh. No, nothing more," Claire says, and once the bellman leaves, we run and jump on the king-sized bed. Then we look at one another and shout in unison, "The bathroom!"

We rush to the marble-covered room and try to squeeze through the doorway at the same time. My mouth drops. The bathroom is about the size of my bedroom/garage. I lower myself onto the edge of the double-sized bathtub. I was jealous when Claire got a Mustang to drive. I was jealous when she got to go hang out at the country club when I went to work. I was jealous when she got new school clothes every year and my mother let down the hem on my homemade pants again. I've been jealous, but this . . . the beauty and simplicity of the room, the view of the famous Recoleta cemetery from the bathroom . . .

"I was born to be rich," I say forlornly.

"You were born to share in it, that's for certain. You'll be back," Claire says brightly.

My dad's in the doorway, and he appears decimated by my comment.

"It's beautiful here, Claire," I say. "I hope you enjoy it, and be safe, all right?" I climb out of the giant bathtub and give her a hug.

"Claire, you have our cell phone number, and we've made sure it works here, so be certain to call us for anything you need. Even if you want company for dinner, is that clear?"

"Yes, Mr. Crispin."

"Okay." I try to keep the whine from my voice. "We'd better go."

"Already?"

"My mom will be grilling Max. I suppose I have to go rescue him."

We walk back into the massive suite.

"Are you really going to leave?"

"Trust me, I don't want to leave here."

"So don't," Claire says simply, and she turns so my father can't see her face. "You're always doing something for someone else. What is so wrong about taking a vacation? When is it your turn?"

"I'll get my turn after the mission trip." I don't want to say to Claire that some people never get their turn. Certainly most people don't get their turn in this kind of place, but I can't help but want to go easy on her. She may seem spoiled, but the fact is, she's always left on her own. My own parents came along to make certain she'd be safe. Maybe my parents are overprotective, but Claire's seem to want to pay her to go away.

She nods her head, trying to keep her tears at bay.

"Claire, we'll be here tomorrow night for dinner if you don't have plans," my dad says. "We'll take you somewhere nice. How does that sound?"

Claire can't speak, so she nods to my dad.

"Six sound okay? You'll be back from your sightseeing by then?"

She nods again.

"I'll leave a message at the front desk about what Mrs. Crispin and I are doing each day, and you're welcome to join us. I know we may not be the height of fun in your book, but you're always welcome." My dad stretches out his arm toward me. "Come on, Daisy, we have a long drive to get to the mission station, and you'll want to see it before dark."

"You gonna be okay?" I ask Claire.

"Don't." She waves her hands in the air. "I just need to sleep. I'm all choked up, but I'll be fine. I'll book a spa treatment first thing in the morning and I'll be fine."

"Call my parents if you need anything, all right?"

"I'll be fine. I've got my laptop, so I can Skype with Sarika or Angie if I get lonely. After I look up the time change."

"Perfect."

My dad opens the door to the hallway and we say goodbye. Claire shuts the door slowly.

"It's a beautiful room, huh, Dad?" I ask him.

"It's a lot of beautiful rooms. Claire's parents sure are generous with her."

"Maybe, but I'm glad you're here with me," I say honestly.

My dad pushes the elevator button and smiles. The way he does when I know he's really proud of me.

I can almost hear the funeral march as we silently ride the elevator, enter the gold foyer, and exit the doors to the car park, where Max's beat-up white van looks like a wart on the beautiful hand of the hotel. I wish I didn't notice such things. I stare into the hotel windows and see a woman with a froufrou dog and a mound of matching luggage, and I hate myself for having to leave Claire here alone.

"You all right?"

"Yeah."

"I'm sorry you're not getting your vacation, Daisy. I wish now I'd saved more money for your education, but I think this experience will change you for the better."

I hate to hear my dad sound like a failure. "You did save money for my education, remember? Your health intervened, and I praise God we had the money available for you. Dad, you work hard to make a living at something that makes people happy. Maybe not me, but it makes people happy."

My dad laughs and puts his arm around my shoulder. "You!"

"Besides, if you paid, I wouldn't get to go to such a great school."

"If you're trying to make me feel better, you can stop now."

"I mean, a full, four-year scholarship and only two weeks of mission work in the summers? That's not such a bad deal." But I worry that I'll probably still have to work another week at the food bank to get documentation.

"You've got a good attitude, Daisy. That will take you further than any education."

I wish I had a better attitude. Just because my legs are walking toward the van doesn't mean my heart isn't back in that suite.

Max gets out of the van and helps me into it. Max. What am I to make of him? He pulls me back slightly and asks me quietly, "Can you have dinner with me?"

"When?"

"Tonight, before your work starts."

"Wouldn't that be considered rude to show up and then leave?"

He shrugs. "Can't you make an excuse? Otherwise I won't see you at all."

"Why not?"

"Tell them you've got jet lag, and I'll pick you up at six."

"Lie?"

"Oh no, you'll have jet lag."

"What are you two whispering about?" my father asks.

"Dinner," I announce bluntly. "Max and I are going out to dinner tonight. After I get settled in and receive my initial instructions. I'll have all day tomorrow to prepare for Vacation Bible School."

"Is it safe?"

"Dad, look at this place!" I noticed earlier that everything is so clean and cultured. The buildings are traditional and important-looking, as if there are heads of states and royalty residing within. "It's like a provincial village."

"Appearances can be deceiving, and we're not at the camp yet," my dad says. "Your mother's roommate was bare bones and all business. I can't imagine she's living in the lap of luxury."

I hate feeling so torn. I want to be with Claire. I want to be with Max. I even want to be with my parents. The last thing I want to do is enter another foreign environment with people I don't know.

"Your dad is right," Max admits to my chagrin. "Let's get on the road." He comes around the van and jumps into the driver's seat. "I wouldn't take her out in Escobar. We'll eat somewhere nice in Las Canitas." Max glances at me. "It's the fashionable spot for foodies. You'll love it." He backs out. "It's got expensive little boutiques and the biggest polo field in the city. Where they have the big games in November and December."

"Polo, Dad! They play polo there. I'll be safe."

My dad grimaces at me.

"It's just dinner, Daddy. I'll be away at college in less than two months. Can't you just imagine I'm already there?"

"Is that supposed to make me feel better? At least you speak the language in Malibu. You know the price of something. What if something happens? How do I reach you? I'll have no idea where you are and—and if you don't come back."

Max taps the steering wheel. "How about this? We'll all go to dinner together. How's that?"

I have to close my mouth for fear of swallowing flies. Max's way of solving this problem is not kosher.

"Sounds wonderful," my mom says. "We wanted to have a nice dinner out and not just eat in the hotel both weeks, right, honey?"

"I did promise Claire we'd go out tomorrow night," my dad says.

"Oh," my mom says, no doubt doing calculations in her head. "But it does sound so nice. Max, being local, would know of a good restaurant, and I'm certain it wouldn't be too expensive, right, Max?"

It sounds wonderful to my parents. Well, so does a chastity belt. That doesn't make it right.

"I know of just the place."

I hear myself sigh out loud.

"Don't you want us to go?" Dad asks me.

"If you change your shirt, maybe."

"We're leaving the Recoleta barrio," Max announces. "This is Palermo. It's the largest of the neighborhoods."

"Look at those skyscrapers," Dad says. "It's like New York."

"SoHo," Max clarifies. "It's young and hip. Where all the

trendy folks live after a day at the office. It's not really for families."

"It's very green, though," my mother says.

"It is," Max says. "A lot of parks here and fruit trees and vineyards. Maybe like your Napa a little bit?"

I slink farther into the van's cloth seats. I'm not really in the mood for the whirlwind tour of Buenos Aires, as I'm currently trying to decide how to lose my parents from my impending date.

Dad takes out his camera and snaps a few photos of the lush area when we stop at lights. "What's that there?"

"That's the Lagos de Palermo—the lakes. The zoo is here, and the Japanese gardens as well. I guess it's kind of a city center. Hopefully you'll get a chance to tour this area. There's a world-famous planetarium too. I think you're going to have a great time while you're here."

"Sounds like Golden Gate Park," Dad says.

"Maybe," Max says. "But you'll see that everything here has a different feel, maybe slightly more artistic, no?"

"Ah yes, and there's the historical aspect that's so much richer than anything we have in California," my father says.

Max laughs. "Now we're heading into Las Canitas, where we'll have dinner."

I pout through the entire barrio, but do my parents get the message?

"Well, that looks lovely," Mom says. "We should have a nice meal here. I hope Libby hasn't planned anything for us. Max, we will have to beg off the invitation if Libby has dinner planned. We wouldn't want to be rude."

"Goes without mentioning. This is Belgrano," Max continues, and truthfully, I'm grateful for the buzzing noise of

Max's narration that keeps my mom and dad content. "It's an upscale neighborhood, and it used to be the government center, so there are a lot of military statues, that kind of thing. Very official-looking, don't you think?"

"The buildings are beautiful," I say, to see if anyone can hear me.

"The row houses look like something out of San Francisco," Mom says. "Everything is so neat and clean. It's like Disneyland. Look at the cobblestone streets there. Don't you think it looks like Disneyland, Daisy?"

"If you say so." I cross my arms and look out the other window. It's hard to enjoy your first international vacation when you're touring it like a five-year-old with your parents. Yeah, I'm happy they came, but could they not let me just have had the car ride? Was that too much to ask? At least they didn't bring the leash like they did when they took me to the Grand Canyon.

Max pulls the van over to the side of the road and stops. He turns to face me. "Daisy, you're such a sensitive soul. I need to prepare you for the real Buenos Aires. We're going to the part that people don't usually see. Once you leave the tourist areas, it can be harsh."

"Max, it's poor. I understand. That's why I'm here."

He shakes his head. "I don't know if you do understand. Poor compared to St. James's students isn't poor. Not having enough to feed your family or warm clothes and bedding for them at night? That's poor."

Hasn't Max been to my house? If there's something I'm familiar with, it's poverty in the midst of mass riches. "I'm fine, Max."

Dad twists around and gets that deep expression on his

face. The one he usually has before I get a sermon. "You haven't seen this kind of poverty, Daisy. The reason your sponsors wanted you to see something like this is so that you'll truly understand the gift you've been given and that much will be expected. Finance doesn't mean a thing if you don't understand the human costs."

"I get it. Quit looking at me." Don't they think I'm worried about it for myself? I am. It's going to pain me to see children without enough. Hearing about it is only making my anxiety grow.

Max's cell phone rings, and he answers it. "*Hola.*" He rambles on so quickly that I understand only the fifth or sixth word. *Madre*, meaning "mother," is one of them. His voice pleads, but he seems to agree at the end. "*Sí. Sí. Sí!*" He punches a button and puts his foot to the gas again. "I'm afraid dinner will have to wait. I'm needed at home."

"Oh," my mom says. "Well, that's too bad. Isn't that too bad, Daisy?"

Max reaches into his bag between the front seats. "I brought something for you." He hands me lice shampoo and automatically I scratch my head.

"Are you trying to tell me something?"

"Just for protection. You don't want to bring lice back to Claire's hotel."

"I don't want to bring lice anywhere. There's going to be lice?"

"And maggots and kids without shoes or food."

I suddenly understand the gravity of what he's telling me, and I'm not sure I am ready. As we exit the freeway, we see a mother juggling with one hand and balancing a baby on her hip. She nearly jumps in front of our van to extend her hand for money. Max swings around her and exits the thoroughfare.

The smooth road underneath us disappears, and the bumpy dirt path jiggles us all over. I grasp the armrest to stay in the seat. My mood drops as if I can feel the sadness in the air. The needs seem so overwhelming that I wonder if I can make even the smallest dent by coming here.

The bright green grasses and the perfectly ordered mansions and skyscrapers are long gone. In their wake are makeshift concrete shacks and mud everywhere. The smell of the dirt hits my nostrils first, and as I get accustomed to it, deeper, more vile smells infiltrate. The stench is awful, like mud combined with a dirty river and sewage. I cover my nose with my sleeve as we go farther into what looks like a battle zone.

There are children everywhere, like cattle roaming free on a plain. They are little, unguarded, and filthy. Most of them have shaved heads, and I circle my hand around the lice shampoo.

My breathing is shallow. Max pulls the van up to the address on my paperwork, and it looks like an abandoned building. My heart is in my throat as I think about getting left here alone. It's ominous in nature, isolated . . . bare.

"It doesn't look like there's anyone here. Are you sure this is the right address, Max?" I ask him.

"It's the right address," my dad says, reading the brochure. "Libby told your mother it was humble. And if she said humble, I instinctively took a few amenities off."

"Libby takes humble to a new level," Max says.

"She said it was humble or invisible? I feel like I'm in a horror movie and the place might disappear in the mist. Or in the dirt cloud from the van."

Children rush to the van, and Max gets out and speaks to them. He hands out little pieces of candy he's brought with him.

"I'll go meet Libby." My mom unlatches her seat belt and covers my hand with her own. "It will be fine, Daisy. Libby wouldn't allow you to be put in danger. You should feel honored the needs are such that you won't get bored while you're here."

"I'm not afraid," I lie. I keep hoping that if I think *bravery* often enough, it will make it so.

My mom and dad exit the van and Max opens the back doors. "I didn't want you to see this part of my country. No one should have to live like this."

"Maybe if I get good enough at finance, fewer people will have to live like this."

"If anyone can do it, it would be you."

I lean my chin on my arm. "You really can't do dinner tonight?"

He shakes his head. "My mom was adamant. She needs me for something and wouldn't tell me what it was, only that it was vital."

"Will I see you before I leave here?"

He looks at the shack in front of him. "I'll try to come back tonight and bring you a few more things. It looks like you might like to have some things that make you feel more at home. Snacks, maybe?"

"That would be great." I calculate when my parents will leave for their hotel and the possible discussion Max and I might have under the full moon, and instantly I remember my promise to Claire that I will not romanticize a futile friendship in a foreign country.

"Just like you didn't want me to see this part of your country, I didn't want you to see my house. How about if we make a deal not to hold each other responsible for things we have nothing to do with?"

"Deal."

I climb out of the van and round the vehicle to where Max is standing. The neighborhood kids are still milling about, and I feel bad that I didn't know to bring them some sweets. "Maybe you could bring me some candy when you come back. If I give you money?"

He looks at the dirty little faces around us. "Sure."

I open up my wallet and grab a few bills. "Will this be hard to change into your money?"

"Not at all. You're thoughtful." He plants a chaste kiss on my cheek.

Am I thoughtful like an elderly aunt? Because that's what that kiss meant. "I missed you," I tell him.

He smiles at me, and his silence punctures my heart.

"Let me help you with all the luggage. Your parents have a cab coming later?"

"Yes, Libby said she'd find someone to take them back to town. She wanted to reminisce first."

Max places the suitcases on the porch of the sparse, concrete building, a simplistic rectangle.

"You can do anything, Daisy." He squeezes my hand. Max is king of eye contact, but he won't look at me. "You've got the world at your fingertips." His cell phone buzzes and he glances at the text. "I have to run."

I stare at the building. "I wonder if there's a worse feeling than not having a choice, of being powerless."

"There is, Daisy. You'll have to trust me on that." He brushes the back of his hand along my jaw. "I've got to go."

I grasp his wrist with more desperation than I'd planned. "But you'll be back after dinner tonight?"

"I'll do my best." He stares into the distance, slams the back of the van shut, and climbs into the front without a proper goodbye.

"Well, Claire, you should be happy," I say to myself. "Romance is not going to be a part of my Argentine experience. Clearly."

5

My mom rushes out the door. "Daisy! Daisy! Come meet Libby!" She scoops her arm around me and hurtles me toward the door with such force, I have to push back not to run into Libby. "Libby Bramer, this is my daughter, Daisy. Daisy, Ms. Bramer."

"It's nice to meet you," I say. "Thank you so much for letting me do my scholarship requirements here."

Libby is a pale woman and doesn't crack a smile. Her pasty skin matches her hair, and there seems to be no contrast to any of her features, giving her a ghostly pallor. The only color on her is a gauzy cotton skirt in an Indian design and a "Peace" T-shirt. The sixties are alive and well in Libby's world. Next to my mother, she's positively Bohemian.

"You'll receive no favors from me," Libby says. "You do the work or I don't sign off on the paperwork. That goes for anyone who works for me."

"Naturally," I say, taken aback by her abruptness. *Can't you say hello?* I want to ask her.

"Daisy's such a hard worker," Mom says. "You won't have any trouble getting a full day's work out of her. She worked overtime through her whole high school career."

"Why?"

"She was saving for a car to drive at school."

"Humph. Can't you take the bus?" Libby asks me.

"I have taken the bus for many years. I hoped to have my own car in college."

"Seems like a waste of money when the public transportation system works fine."

"Daisy will probably work through school. She'll need to get to work," my mom says.

"It's her money. I don't care what she does with it. I'm only saying it seems like a waste of money. We rode bikes when I went to school. Remember?"

"Ms. Bramer, where should I put my stuff? I'd like to rest for a while. I'm exhausted from the trip."

"Already? How old are you?"

"She's seventeen," Mom says, "but this was her first international flight."

"You'll be out in the classrooms there with the other staff. None of them have showed up yet, but you can go pick out your mattress and toss it on the floor. If you need a sleeping bag, they're in the cabinet next to the chalkboard. I'll go unlock the room." Libby takes a ring of keys and leads us to the outbuilding behind the smaller rectangle she calls home. She sticks a key in the door and unlocks a deadbolt. "You hungry?"

I'm starving! "No."

"Daisy, you need to eat," Mom says.

"I think I'm too nervous to eat."

A horn honks steadily. "Oh, that's Hank. He'll be driving you to your hotel," Libby says. My dad is standing by quietly—trying to stay out of Libby's way, perhaps?

"So soon?" Mom asks. "I thought we might help Daisy get settled."

"She's a big girl. She can't make her own bed?"

"Mom, I'll be fine. You and Dad go and have a nice dinner and I'll talk to you at the end of the work week."

I can tell my mother's bear sense has kicked in and she does not want to leave me with Libby just yet. Something tells me my dad is going to get a big dose of being right when they get to the hotel. He should enjoy that.

"What are you smiling about, Daisy?" Dad asks me.

"Just thinking about how much fun I'm going to have with the kids."

He winks at me, runs to get my bag, and sets it down outside the dilapidated building. He kisses my cheek. "Be good. You have our cell number if you need anything." He looks at Libby. "If Daisy needs us, I'll reimburse you for any phone calls she makes."

"Naturally," Libby says.

The horn blares again. My mom kisses my cheek and wraps me in an anaconda-like grip. "Call us if you need anything," she whispers into my ear.

I nod.

Libby claps her hands. "Chop chop. Hank can't wait forever. No time for dramatic goodbyes. She'll be fine. Or she won't, and this wasn't the job for her."

My parents are shuffled off like unwelcome relatives, and Libby soon comes back toward me. My mom's eyes are filled with worry as they pull away in the giant sedan.

"Get your rest!" Libby yells at me. "We get up at six sharp around here to get things ready."

I nod and push my suitcase into the lopsided classroom

building. Let me just say, for the record, this was not the warm Latino welcome I was expecting. I should know better than to stereotype.

I pull a mattress down from against the wall and pull out my travel journal. Maybe this will prevent me from making future travel mistakes.

My Life: Stop—July 6, 8:04 p.m.

Random factoid: Al Asador is a traditional Argentine BBQ—and we're not having one.

I wanted to have an experience in Argentina. I wanted to feel the plight of the people so that it might drive me to fulfill my calling in finance and not become a selfish hoarder. However, starving was not what I had in mind. At least not on the first night. I rummaged through the cabinets, hoping to find something to cook on the warming plate, but unless I want to make melted crayon art, I am plumb out of luck. The more I try to think about not being hungry, the louder my stomach gets. If I could only put aside my pride and go knock on Libby's door . . . but I can't. Quite simply, my host scares me.

Oh, the agony!

The classroom is festive, with a colorful mural of Jesus on a mountain, arms outstretched and little children of every color sitting at his feet. The cabinets are all painted in bold, vibrant colors, and the room itself is happy, making me hopeful for what the week will bring.

It does have its creepy aspects, don't get me wrong. A long rectangle of a room with chipped concrete on the floor, walls, and ceiling. I've pulled out my filthy, most likely infested mattress and thrown it on the concrete floor, and I'm ready for bed. I already had a nap and awoke in the damp, cold air to the moist scent of beans and rice, taunting me with their glorious smell. I wonder if I will look back at this journal and think how stupid I was not to just get up, march over to the kitchen, and get some food. Only the future will tell.

Since I came down here with romantic hopes, I think it's only fair that I write down what happened with Max. Except I don't really know, other than he dumped me for dinner after a phone call from his mama. This means he's either (1) a mama's boy or (2) a liar. Or maybe (3) he's just not interested, and if that's the case, he should not have flirted with me on Skype and lured me down here. Maybe that was a boost to his ego. So if my thirty-five-year-old self is reading this, please tell me that you aren't this pathetic. That you learned something from this humiliation.

"Daisy, are you asleep?"

I bounce from my mattress and clamber out of my sleeping bag. "No, no, I'm not asleep. Is Max here? He was going to bring me some treats for the children."

I'm struck again by Libby, a stern, colorless woman. It's like her hair, her face, her features—they all blend into one bland color, and nothing strikes you about her except the assault of her bluntness. She doesn't have the warmth of what I imagined a missionary to have, and her personality seems more like a Silicon Valley CEO than a ministry-running missionary in a third-world country.

"Max?" she asks. "Who's that?"

"No one. A friend from school, is all."

"I wanted to check if your friend from Pepperdine had arrived."

"My friend?"

"The other scholarship recipient from Pepperdine."

"I didn't realize there was another recipient."

"Yes, when she heard where you were going on the mission, she signed up for the same work. I suppose so she'd have a connection once she got to the school. That should be nice for both of you. So this Max? He lives here?"

"Max is a friend of mine who lives in Buenos Aires."

"You kids with your internet. You're world travelers without getting out of your beds."

I venture a smile.

"I'll put a sign on the door and send the other student out here tonight. It's always good to have a connection before meeting the kids. If the other volunteer doesn't show up tonight, I'll send the dog out to sleep with you."

I've seen that dog. "No, it's all right. I'll be fine. I sleep in the garage at home, so I'm used to this."

"I don't want you to be out here alone. It's for my own peace of mind. Lot of work to do tomorrow, so you'll want to get your rest." Libby lifts a clipboard from the wall. "It looks like your shower day will be Thursday. You brought a towel and your own toiletries like the listing required?"

"I did, but today's Wednesday."

"I mean of next week. We've already taken our allotment today. You look pretty clean to me. Besides, the dirt protects you."

"From?"

She just shrugs. My attitude is definitely not that of a good, serving missionary. It's more Claire-like at the moment, and how I wish I'd stayed there in her luxurious suite to bathe in that giant marble bathtub before I'd left. A week? I am going to be riper than a California raisin.

"We'll have breakfast at seven a.m., and then we'll start training. The kids will be milling about everywhere tomorrow, and they'll be so excited to get started. So I need you to keep your mind on your job and working with the girls who know the ropes. With the language barrier, you're going to be partnered with a translator."

I nod and force a smile. Something about the woman rubs me the wrong way. As if this may be her best behavior. Isn't that awful? Maybe it's because so far she's broken every manner rule my mother—and her friend—ever taught me during our introduction. It's like she's devoid of human emotion. I want to find that place of connection within her, but at the same time I want to avoid her with all that I am.

"I want you to understand that I run a tight ship. As I said earlier, if everything is to my satisfaction at the end of Vacation Bible School, I will sign off on your papers and the scholarship will be yours."

I veer back slightly at her words. It never occurred to me

that this was some kind of test. I imagined I'd come down here and get the work done and be on my way to Malibu.

"You're surprised. You shouldn't be. You wouldn't believe how many kids come down here for some kind of spring break experience rather than to do the work God has called them to. I'm here to ensure that doesn't happen. This work is my life calling. I can't be babysitting short-time do-gooders if I'm going to be effective here for the long haul. The kids have to know they must show respect here. You'd be surprised how out of control things get when chaos reigns."

"Well, isn't that the definition of chaos? Ms. Bramer, I can assure you, I think my parents would tell you—"

She laughs. "Parents often miss their children's flaws. Not having any of my own children, I rarely miss the flaws."

My body involuntarily shudders. "I'm really tired from my traveling. I need to go back to bed if I have to rise at six."

"If you need to use the outhouse tonight, I'll leave a lantern here by the door. Don't leave it outside or it will get stolen and you'll have no way back. Everything here can be sold, so don't leave anything out, and don't venture off without a translator. You may think you know Spanish, but if you get into trouble, words will fail you."

I slide into my sleeping bag again. "Okay, thanks. See you in the morning."

There's no more mention of the dog or the other missionary, and Libby slinks out backwards, turns off the light, and pulls the door shut with force. I'm left in the pitch-black darkness with no more colorful reminders of children's paintings on the wall. I have that prickly feeling that bugs are in my hair, which I'm sure is only my imagination.

I'm not sure how long I'm asleep before I'm awakened

by the door slamming against the wall. Groggily, I call out, "Who's there?"

A male voice answers, and I tighten my bag around me. "J.C. Wiggs. Who's there?" he answers in English.

"Daisy Crispin. There's a lantern there next to the door. Feel to your left." But he finds the light switch and burns my retinas. "Ouch!"

"Sorry. I guess that's why you mentioned the lantern."

I blink slowly as my sight returns and look at J.C., who can only be described as . . . missing from a boy band somewhere. He's blond-haired with prominent cheekbones that I can make out in the shadows. He's got a messenger bag strapped across his torso, which is muscular and stretching his T-shirt to its proverbial limit. I, on the other hand, look like Marley's ghost, and worse yet, I smell like him. Apparently I will continue to do so for a week. Or until I make my escape to Claire's suite. Whichever comes first.

"I'm sorry. I woke you, obviously." He shuts off the overhead light and turns on the lantern. I watch him twist his wrist and check his watch, and even in the shadows, he's like someone from an Armani ad. Life isn't fair. Guys can fly all night and look like that. "It's only ten o'clock. Most people don't eat dinner down here until then."

"I've got jet lag. Arrived today from California. I've been sleeping since around five."

"Ah."

"Where are you from?" I sit up in my sleeping bag and mat down my hair, grateful for the darkness. For all I know, I could look like Jessica Biel in this light. Then again, for all I know just because he looks like a teen idol doesn't mean he isn't a serial killer stalking the barrio streets. Of course, he does speak English. And he's cute, so the fear won't come, hard as I try to summon some.

"Arizona," he answers. "Some woman told me to come out here and sleep." He holds up a note next to the lantern. "It's not exactly the Latino welcome I imagined."

"That's exactly what I said! But Libby isn't Latino."

"Libby?"

"She runs the mission."

"Right. She must think I'm a girl," he said.

"I think you're right from what she told me."

"Well, I've been on a few summer mission trips, and they never let the guys sleep in the same quarters as the girls."

"You can sleep over there." I point to the opposite side of the room. "I won't touch you, I promise." Even if daily rejection is my middle name.

He laughs and lifts his pack from outside the door. "So you haven't done this before, I take it?"

"Is it obvious?"

"You just have no expectations. That's how you're supposed to come on a mission, but it never works like that. It's always worse and better than you imagine."

"What does that mean?"

"The place is always worse. The people you help, always better than you imagine."

"Ah."

He pulls out a bag from his pack and my mouth waters at the mere thought of food. I lick my lips. "You hungry?"

I can't even be demure at this point. "I'm starving—famished, really. Do you have enough?"

"Plenty."

"There's a table over in that corner." I climb out of my

sleeping bag, grateful I'm wearing yoga-like pants and a long T-shirt, but wishing my hair wasn't flying every which way. I'm not even thinking romance either, just self-respect. J.C. is what I'd consider out of my league.

But as I step closer to J.C., my confidence wanes. Luckily hunger rules my vanity. We both sit at the table, and he smiles at me from over the lantern. He takes a sandwich out of the bag and rips it in half. "I hope you don't mind my fingers. My mom sent me with a crapload of hand sanitizer, so they're clean. She was frantic I was going to come home with the plague."

"She sounds a lot like my parents, only they came with me. They're staying in town at a hotel."

"You're kidding me. I thought no one could outparent my mother, but they're here? Really?"

"My mom went to college with Libby. I guess that was their excuse, but I'm still seventeen, so that was their other excuse. Though I'm sure if I were eighteen, they would have found another one."

"We definitely have to get our parents together at orientation."

"Are you kidding? Do you want them sharing notes?"

J.C. laughs. "Good point."

I grab my half of the sandwich and shove it into my mouth. I mumble over the food, "Sorry, I'm eating like a cavewoman."

He grins and he has one dimple on his right side, which makes him even more out of my league. I appreciate this because it takes the pressure off.

"It's refreshing. I've had too many dates where the girl won't eat. Nice to see one with a healthy appetite."

"So you're going to Pepperdine too?" I grab his soda. "Do you mind?"

"Be my guest."

I slurp from the bottle and hand it back to him.

"They didn't feed you when you got here?" he asks.

"Long story. I was supposed to go out with my boyfriend. Ex-boyfriend? Friend? I'm not sure what exactly he is, but he had to go back home, and I thought I could make it through the night rather than ask Libby for food."

"Is she that bad?"

"No. Yes. I don't really know. I just felt self-conscious and didn't want to ask her for anything."

"That doesn't sound good."

"Max said he'd come back to bring me some candy for the kids and I thought I'd just eat some of that, but I guess he got busy. I gave him some money. I wonder if he had trouble exchanging it."

"No offense, but he sounds like a jerk."

"I don't think so. Something's up, but I don't think he's a jerk."

"Girls always say that when the guy's a dog."

I snort a laugh. "Sorry." I cover my mouth. "But you're probably right. My background isn't exactly filled with success stories."

"Neither is mine, if you want the truth. My girlfriend broke up with me because if I loved her, I would have gone to Arizona State."

"And why didn't you?"

"Because I got into Pepperdine. If she loved me, she'd want me to go where I wanted to go."

"Maybe love is too complicated."

"Nope. It's women who are too complicated."

"That's how it is too. Guys are never to blame."

"I'm glad you get it. Where have you been all my life?"

I slap him in the arm.

"I heard you got the other scholarship. How'd you raise enough money to get down here? My grandmother fronted mine, which isn't exactly raising capital, but it sounded like such a great opportunity and I thought I could use my Spanish down here, so I signed on as soon as I heard. I already had my local food bank sign off on one week, though."

"No way! You work at your local food bank? I do too and already put in a week," I say, once again over a bite of food. He's probably thinking I could eat my local food bank.

The door slams open and Libby is standing there with a flashlight in one hand and a baseball bat in the other.

"J.C., meet Libby Bramer."

"J.C.'s a boy?" Libby rushes into the room and grabs J.C. by the collar. "You're supposed to be a girl. It says 'female' on your paperwork."

"I don't think it does," J.C. says.

"It must. Or I wouldn't have approved your application. We have nowhere to house you. All of the rest of the volunteers this session are female."

J.C. looks at me. "Should I apologize for being male?" he says under his breath.

"He shared his sandwich with me," I offer. It seemed reasonable before I said it.

"Daisy, get in the house. You can sleep upstairs in the loft. Bring your sleeping bag. You'll sleep out here," Libby says to J.C. as if he's some kind of predator.

Somehow I pictured my first mission experience being more

holy than this. I spend my life feeling perpetually in trouble, and the really annoying aspect of this is that I rarely do anything worthy of guilt. I'm feeling troublesome. Like if I'm going to get into trouble anyway, maybe I should just cause it and have the fun to make it worth my while.

Libby's not finished with me. "I can't believe you didn't come in and tell me. Your parents said they raised you right. You were going to sleep out here? With a boy you don't know?"

"I was just—"

"No, no excuses. Get into the house and we'll discuss this in the morning. I'd like to talk to J.C. alone."

With a screech of his chair, J.C. stands up. "No, you have it wrong, Ms. Bramer. Daisy told me I couldn't sleep here. I asked if I could eat my dinner first, in case the rogue dogs came around. Then I planned to go outside on the porch."

Libby crosses her arms. "Well." She clears her throat. "I'm sorry. I misspoke, but you can understand I can't have things questioned when parents trust me with their children."

"Naturally. No reason to be upset. Let me know what I can do to make things run smoother for you and I'll do it," J.C. purrs like a kitten. To my shock, it works on Libby.

"Get a good night's sleep and be in the main house promptly at seven for breakfast. Daisy, gather your things and meet me in the house."

"Right away, ma'am."

With all the grace of a typhoon, Libby exits the classroom, and the space feels calmer.

"I've seen Libby's type before," J.C. says. "Just do as she says and stay out of her way. If you stay under the radar, she'll sign off on your mission. Don't take anything she says personally, or she's won."

I nod. "What choice do we have? I won't have time to fulfill another mission requirement before school starts."

"That's just the kind of power her sort thrives on," J.C. said. "Don't be afraid of her. She can sense fear."

"Why do I feel like I'm embarking on a combat mission?"

"Because you are, Daisy." J.C. salutes me and I crumble into a giggle. "Private J.C. Wiggs reporting for duty, sir!"

I salute back. "We're going to make the best of this."

"Darn straight we are."

I leave the classroom with a smile and just a tad more dignity.

6

"Daisy, isn't that bed made yet?" Libby shouts at me, and my body instinctively straightens.

"It's made," I say, because let's face it, she scares me. She'd scare a pit bull. And though my body was weak from travel fatigue at six o'clock, I instinctively popped up out of my cot and rolled my sleeping bag like I was in boot camp. It makes me wish I possessed more of Claire's boldness in life.

I climb down the ladder from the loft that served as my bedroom for the night. My stomach clenches at the sight of Libby, who I'm sure is a lovely person and accomplishes much in the third world, but that doesn't make her my BFF.

Inside her house, the walls are whitewashed and the few furnishings are sparse, don't match, and are all arranged in a particular order that brings a rustic, homey quality to the room. On either side of the rectangular room there is a loft in each corner, both of which are no more than wooden landings with room enough for beds. There is no privacy in the house, and I wonder what it's like to have people come in and out for ministry—it reminds me of *Little House on the Prairie*. The lofts are reached by rickety, bamboo-like ladders. I'm certain it's not bamboo, but it hardly matters, and like J.C. says, I want to stay under the radar, so I don't ask. Something tells me Libby doesn't want to offer decorating advice anyway.

My particular loft will sleep two, though there's only one cot, and the other loft is Libby's bedroom and has an old cotton mattress of sorts, piled with blankets. I "made my bed" by rolling it back into a ball and hiding it under my cot.

Libby calls down to me from her cot again. "Daisy, I've got water on the stove, so would you add the oatmeal to it once it comes to a full boil? Add a little sugar too, or it never seems to get sweet enough, and you kids use a week's supply."

I pad over to the stove on the cool cement floor and see that the water is already boiling. The cardboard tube of oats is right beside the stove. It's got the Quaker on it and everything, but reads *avena tradicional* instead of whatever it reads in America. I open the container and realize I have no idea how much to add, but the idea of being snapped at for being useless keeps me quiet. I assume Libby will find the fact that I can't make oatmeal another character flaw on my parents' part, so I just pour in the oats and pray for the best.

"Daisy!" Libby shouts.

I look up and her ghostly face peers down at me. There's something distant in the way she looks right through me. There's rejection, certainly, but there's something missing inside of Libby Bramer, and it feels impossible to really connect with her. It's something I can't put my finger on but keeps her preoccupied in her mind while her mouth spews obligations and rules. It makes me want to find the part of her that has devoted her life to the children of Argentina. I know it's in there somewhere.

"Did I put too much in?" I ask her.

She looks at the pot. "It's fine. The door. Get the door. Are you deaf?"

I give the oatmeal a stir, head to the rustic front door, and unlatch the two-by-four that serves as a lock like on a medieval castle. Three guys straight out of Argentina's *GQ* face me. "The rest of the boy band are here."

"Pardon?" Libby asks.

"Just a joke!" I call out. I open the door wider so that she can see the three model-like guys standing on her cement stoop. Does Buenos Aires have any ugly guys? And with the bounty that's before me, why am I still obsessing about where Max is? Maybe this is one of those "when God closes a door, he opens a window" kind of things. The view from this window is astounding.

My mind wanders to Max and what might have possibly kept him from coming back the previous night, and what it all means. It's that closure thing again. If I'm going to be dumped, I at least request the decency of being dumped properly, am I right? Simple respect, which puts me back in the moment.

"I'm sorry," I finally say to the group of three young men. *Tres amigos*. "Welcome. You're here to work?"

"We're the translators for the Vacation Bible School," the tallest of them says in a thick accent. "I assume you're American."

"How can you tell?"

"Sneakers." He looks down at my feet.

"You're supposed to be female!" Libby shouts from the loft,

and the three of them stare at me as if I've rejected them. I just shrug. How can I possibly make excuses for Libby?

"That's Libby. She's in charge, and she was under the impression she had a female staff this time. Right now it's looking like the opposite except for me."

"Ah," the tallest says as he looks up to see Libby. "Our church is having a women's retreat this weekend. No women available."

"Come on in. I'm cooking oatmeal for breakfast and we'll prepare for the week." I open the door wider and they walk in one by one. "I'm Daisy Crispin, from California."

"Oscar Sosa," the tall one says. "From Argentina." He has one of those furry lips that isn't quite a mustache and makes me want to rub my finger over the spot and run for the hot wax. He's still gorgeous, but with some simple hygiene, he'd be perfect.

"I'm not going to play chaperone this whole week!" Libby calls, and then noticing that the guys can hear her, she goes back to the side of her bed and opens her Bible. "Lord have mercy! I'm supposed to run the school this week, not keep hormone-fueled kids apart! God, are you hearing me?" she rants.

While Libby's talking to herself or expressing her disappointment with God, it's beyond awkward as the guys stand in front of me, probably not remotely interested in me, and certainly not fighting any urge to get closer.

"*Hola*," says the second one with a black waterfall of sexy curls. "Jose Palovar from Chile. I apologize for not being female. I'll talk to my parents about it."

I smile at his comment. "You do that. I also think we can manage to keep our hands to ourselves, but I know I'm a lot to take in." I laugh, but I'm not sure he understands that I'm joking. My humor doesn't translate, apparently.

I realize the scent of oatmeal isn't all that welcoming. It smells a bit like stale cheese in the makeshift cottage. For me, it brings up too many memories of welcoming people into my mother's messy, craft-making lair. I feel that same sense of shame wash over me. I realize that shame shouldn't be mine, but I'm embarrassed all the same.

Just once I'd like to "meet cute" instead of the series of humiliating introductions that happen to me. Just once, is that too much to ask?

The third guy follows after the other two, and my breath catches at the sight of him. He has those ice-blue eyes that I've seen only on models in perfume commercials. The eyes combined with jet-black hair give him an almost inhuman look. He's the kind of person you can't help but stare at, and I'm sure for him, that's disconcerting. But dang! I wonder what that's like to hover so far above the normal human fray.

"Leo Cristal." He stretches out his hand, but I'm too mesmerized to reach for it. It's not even that I'm interested. He's way too out of my league, but I've never seen someone like him in person. He should be carved into marble and preserved.

"You're a translator?" I say this as if I'm asking him if he can talk too. I try to recover some semblance of dignity. "You look like you should star in vampire movies."

So much for dignity.

"Not much call for that down here." He laughs. "Are you saying I look like a vampire?" He lifts his hands into claws.

How does one explain as a Christian that vampires are very popular right now? That it's a compliment that I think he wants to suck someone's blood?

Vampire movies. Is there really any recovering from that comment?

"Where are you from?" I ask Leo.

"Transylvania," one of his friends answers with a laugh.

Leo is flushed, but his eyes soften as he acknowledges my humiliation. "Believe it or not, I've heard that before, so don't feel bad. You'll have to trust me that I make a better translator than a vampire. A better Christian too, and I'm a vegetarian." He grins. "I'm from right around here. Just a few miles up the road."

"Daisy, what are you talking about vampires for? What do they teach you in that Christian high school of yours? It's like I say, America is on the fast track to trouble." Libby stops and stares down at the stove. "Get to that oatmeal before it bubbles over," she says, and I suddenly feel like Cinderella.

I walk to the stove and the giant metal pot and begin to stir the thick, bubbling brew. With both hands on the long wooden spoon, it does seem like I could make an incantation over the oatmeal, but I think that would be the final straw for Libby and my dark American ways. I'm on shaky ground as it is. I wish I understood why everyone assumes I'm such trouble before giving me an opportunity to prove myself a nuisance.

Libby climbs down the ladder from her loft. Her hair is straw-colored and without life. She's wearing beige cotton pants and a billowy, shade-of-wheat shirt. In a country full of color, Libby takes bland to an art form. She walks straight up to the three young men and stares them down as if they're all guilty of something.

"I specifically asked for female translators. Does your mission service have trouble telling the difference?"

"The mission group had a shortage of women this month. They figured males would be better than no one," says Oscar, the tallest with the bad mustache.

Libby groans. "It would have been nice if they'd warned me. The accommodations aren't really set up for both male and female workers."

Oscar stares at me. "That won't be a problem if there's only Daisy, right?"

Libby focuses her laser glare on me. "I suppose I can send you back to the hotel with your parents. We can make do with one less."

"But Libby, I came all the way from California to fulfill my scholarship requirements."

She gives me a cursory glance and goes back to speaking. "As I was saying, I guess God has decided the team will be all male this time."

"Libby, you don't need to make Daisy leave," Oscar says. "I'm certain we can all control ourselves. She's like our little sister. Right, guys?"

I realize they are trying to stand up for me, but to be so quick to call me a little sister isn't doing anything for my already bruised ego. Is it wrong to wish they had the decency to pretend that they're salivating and will control themselves no matter how hard it is?

Libby purses her lips. "If we're going to be male this week, maybe you should go and stay with your parents, Daisy. That would be the sacrificial thing to do."

"It totally would be, but then I don't meet my scholarship requirements and have nowhere to go in the fall. I think you'll agree college is something I can't forgo, no matter how generous I'm feeling."

"Why didn't you think of all this ahead of time?"

"I did!" I say with too much force. "But the letter didn't arrive until late, and by then my summer was already planned. We got out of high school fairly late, and college starts early, so there wasn't a lot of time. Do you want to sign off on the paperwork?"

"Not if you don't meet the requirements. Are you asking me to lie for you?"

"No, of course not. But I'm anxious to help here, and I'm not sure what else to do. It's hardly my fault the team turned out to be male."

"Life is never fair, Daisy. The sooner you learn that lesson, the easier your life will be."

"Please, I need the credits for school!"

This is my punishment for wanting a luxurious vacation rather than simply taking the time to work at my church's food bank. I know it is. If I hadn't wanted it all and just accepted the scholarship and been content, none of this would have happened. I wouldn't have wasted a trip half-way around the world to be dumped by Max and put my scholarship at risk.

"That's unfortunate, but Daisy, you understand I'll have a hundred children here this week. They have to be my first priority."

"Naturally, but Libby, I think you'd be surprised how well the guys and I could work together, and we might change your mind about mixed teams. You might see an advantage to them."

"I doubt that."

"My parents can come stay and chaperone if you're worried about that." I regret this the second it pops out of my mouth.

"There's no room for your parents, Daisy. That's why they left in the first place."

"Not even out in the classroom?"

"No."

Feeling more desperate, I start to panic. "Leo, you're not going to be overcome by passion for me while you translate, am I right? Couldn't I just sleep on the porch?"

Leo laughs. "You're a beautiful girl, but we're here to work."

"Do you see?" Libby says. "He acknowledges you're beautiful, and the fact that he notices renders you useless."

"He was being polite!" I counter. He's so out of my league, can't she see that? If not, I suggest she get thee to an optometrist. "I need this, and I'm good with kids, Libby. I'll be too busy to think about guys. What can I do to prove it to you?"

She stares at me, her beady eyes calculating all that I'm capable of doing with my pure animal magnetism. Ha!

"Every summer these kids rifle in here for the free food and plastic toys at the end of the day, and we've got that one chance to hit 'em with the gospel. I don't want the leaders being sidetracked by any Latino love moves, you got it?"

"We want the same thing!" I say. And to their credit, the guys nod. I'm just praying no one announces they wouldn't touch me with a ten-foot pole. That's a truth I can do without, even if it does spare me my scholarship.

She invades each guy's space and looks directly into their eyes, mere inches from their noses. "Do any of you have divinity school experience?"

Leo, the vampire, nods. "We're all in theology school. We're all about self-control, Libby. I assure you."

"Then I suppose I have no choice but to trust you, but

Daisy, if you want to stay, you need your mother or another female here. I'll be too busy to keep an eye on you, and I'm not going to risk my funding by running a Christian dating service by night."

"Can't I just stay in the house like I did last night?" I ask. "I can't cause any trouble that way, right?"

"I'm sorry, did I stutter?" Libby asks me. "My husband doesn't want to sleep in the car again."

"Your husband?"

"Everybody decent?" Hank, the man who drove my parents to town, sticks his head in the house.

"You're married?"

"That's my husband, Hank."

Hank is a middle-aged man, wide in girth, with a baggy face and a permanent look of worry. I imagine that comes from being married to Libby.

I reach out my hand. "It's nice to meet you. I'm Daisy. Thanks so much for taking my parents to the hotel last night. I had no idea I put you out. I'm so sorry."

"It's no problem, sweetheart. I'm only glad we had a place to put you. Your parents sure are proud of you. A full-ride scholarship. That is really something!"

"She can't have her scholarship if she doesn't complete this mission trip," Leo, my vampire hero, says.

"Good thing you're here then."

I run to the stove to check the oatmeal and turn off the heat. The last thing I need to do is come between Libby and Hank and then, on top of it, burn the oatmeal.

"Hank, Daisy is the only girl on this crew. You know we have no place to house her."

"I'll call my best friend. The two of us can sleep in Hank's car!" I offer, thinking there is probably no chance of Claire checking out of her luxury suite to sleep in a car in the barrio. But I'm desperate.

Libby puts a finger to her chin. "That would work. You know how to reach her?"

"I just have to put a call in at her hotel. She can most likely be here by the end of the day."

And at the same time, we might want to look out for the pigs flying by.

J.C. appears behind Hank in the doorway. "Brrr. Anyone mind if I come in? That classroom is freezing out there. Should I get a fire going?"

"There's no wood for the day," Libby says. "When the kids are here tomorrow, the room will be warm enough from body heat. Daisy, are you watching the oats?"

"I just turned off the heat and stirred them again."

"That's tomorrow. I'm cold now," J.C. says.

"You American kids. All you do is complain. When you see how the kids down here have it, you'll sing a different tune. Put on a sweater."

J.C. opens his mouth—I assume to explain his ministry background—but he shuts it quickly. I think that was the right move. Libby is one of those people who doesn't invite freedom of expression easily.

"May I use the phone to call my friend and see if she can stay?'

"Hank, how do you feel about the girls in your car?"

"Well, terrible. I don't want them to sleep in the car. I can sleep out there. It's only a week."

"No, I want these kids to learn what sacrifice is, and I think it's important that things aren't always done to make their life easier. We have rules here at the mission and they're always the same rules. I can't go changing them because my college roommate's daughter is here."

I stammer a bit and then stand back and point to the phone. "I need to run up to my backpack and get her number."

"You can do that after breakfast. Let's get breakfast cleared up and get on to the day's planning. J.C., I suppose you'll have to lead with the translators, seeing as how we didn't get enough women. I suppose that means you're on cook duty, Daisy."

"Cook duty?" *Have mercy.* I came down to help, not harm. The one time I could really use my parents' help, they are nowhere to be found, and Claire's experience is relegated to calling for takeout. Not that she's going to agree to this fiasco. But one can hope. And pray.

"This may be the only meal those kids get today. It's important work."

"No, I know, I just—" Can't . . . cook.

"Everything is simple enough, you'll be fine. Boys, eat up, we need to get out to the classroom. We're going to have five stations set up when the rest of the local students get here."

"Are they women?"

"It doesn't matter, Daisy, they don't spend the night."

"Maybe I—" I shut my mouth at her expression.

"If we run low on translators, the craft station is the easiest to explain without words." Libby opens a cabinet and pulls down six wooden bowls, then she opens a drawer and takes out mix-and-match spoons. She places them on the table. "You, the tall one—"

"Oscar," he says.

"Oscar, I want you as a witness to what I'm about to say

to all of the volunteers this season, and I'll repeat myself, but I run a tight ship."

"I can see that," Oscar says.

"Serve up the oatmeal, Daisy. We have a long day ahead of us."

Some of us longer than others. I pick up the giant spoon and begin serving the bowls of what I imagine to be crunchy oatmeal. Or maybe just chewy, like wet sawdust. Either way, I think this group of boy band members is not going to be bowled over by my culinary skills, nor excited about a week of eating my cooking, but it's a job that fulfills my requirements and that's all that matters. Now I just have to get Claire or my mother to have mercy on me and join me as Cinderella.

Libby clears her throat. "As you can see, we will probably be shorthanded this week. That means that I expect everyone to pull their own weight, and if you're here for any type of school or community service credit"—she looks right at me when she says this—"I am not a pushover when it comes to signing paperwork. If you want the credit necessary for school, you will do the work, and you will do it to my specifications. Is that clear?"

"She ain't kidding," Hank adds.

She rambles on for some time, and we sit down to eat while she takes Oscar out to the classroom building to get something down for her. I breathe a sigh of relief just by her leaving the room—the air suddenly feels lighter. Hank follows her outside.

"She's a piece of work," J.C. whispers in my ear.

"Shh. She's probably got the place bugged."

"Did you ever hear from your date?"

I shake my head. "It seems coming to Buenos Aires may

have been a bad idea all around. I should have stayed home and worked in my church's food bank. Not only could I have been dumped stateside, but it seems I could have gotten my college credits a lot easier too."

J.C. puts his arm around me. "It will be over before you know it, and we'll be learning to surf in Malibu. Because you know we're just spoiled Americans, might as well live up to our stereotype."

J.C. makes me smile. He hears Libby's voice and drops his arm immediately.

"I hope Max is all right. It's not like him to just disappear without a word." But maybe it is and I haven't faced reality. Maybe I'm meant to be single for the rest of my life, and this is the time to face it so I can concentrate on the life God has for me.

"Really?" J.C. says as if he doesn't believe me, and for a moment I have to wonder.

"I didn't think so. He picked my parents and me up at the airport."

"That was seen."

"Pardon?"

"When people do nice things and it's only stuff that's seen by others? You have to wonder if that's who they really are or if this is who he really is."

"I'm not following."

"My mom's a psychologist, so she talks about this stuff all the time. Maybe Max is really a jerk, but he doesn't want your parents to think that, so he acts right when they're around. Any reason he needs to impress them?"

"Not in the least."

J.C. shrugs. "So maybe I'm wrong. All I can say is that I

wouldn't do that to a girl I liked. Maybe to a girl I was trying to lose, but not to a girl I liked."

"So what does that say about you and your girlfriend? Aren't you going to Pepperdine when she's going to ASU? Are you trying to lose her?"

"No comment, as I fear it might get a cereal bowl thrown at me."

I pick up my bowl of flavorless oatmeal and put it on the table. If this mission trip's aim was to make me feel useless, worthless, and humbled, I think my work is done here. And it hasn't even begun.

7

My Life: Stop—July 7

Factoid: My internship is "illegal," or unregistered, as they call it here. To work legally, I needed to have temporary residence, but because of the short time frame, I was assured this wouldn't be necessary. Well, that and the fact that there's no pay, so what's to quibble about, right?

I've never worked so hard to stay on a vacation in my life, and I'm not even wanting to be on this vacation. My mother's college roommate is a piece of work. Even as I write this, I'm afraid she's looking over my shoulder and looking for an excuse to send me packing.

I left a guilt-ridden (worthy of my mother!) and pleading message for Claire at her hotel, but no doubt she was off learning the tango with some of Argentina's sexiest teenagers and then soothing her tired muscles with a hot rock massage back at the hotel spa.

I also left a message for my mother asking for money. I figure if I can hitch a ride back to their hotel or pay for a closer one, I'd be considered local and Libby would have no choice but to reinstate my missionary status.

Never heard from Max, but here's the really amazing part: I don't care. I'm not even faking it. Being with J.C., who is nothing more than a friend, made me think I always felt terrible when Max left. Even if we'd had this really great time together, I always felt slightly lower when he left. Like I didn't know what to expect the next time. I think in the future I'm going to search out more stable personalities. Like Claire. I mean, she may be perpetually crazy, but the fact is, you can always count on that.

Maybe working for my playboy boss all those years taught me some bad habits. There's nothing wrong with a drama-free existence. Let's face it, Claire provides more drama than anyone needs in life, so I need more of that like I need another guy on this mission trip who looks like a telenovela star.

I think my stomach will be in a perpetual knot until I get out of Libby's presence. If it's possible, I feel like she just resonates this nervous energy that makes me want to jump out of my skin. It makes me long for my toilet-paper-strewn bedroom and the strictness that I understand and—let's face it—that makes more sense. My parents being freaked out because Claire might take us on a wild goose chase in her Mustang is reasonable. Believing every guy currently residing in Argentina is hot for me—not so much.

Even though this is not quite a travel journal and more a place where I spill my pathetic life secrets, I've come to understand that flying across the world has not changed who I am. In fact, it's only made me feel more invisible, as if I can be cast off by Libby Bramer as easily as an old winter coat.

But that's my choice, I figure. I'm not going to let a woman like her make me feel bad. She's miserable by nature. I can't fix that, and truthfully, I don't even want to try. I just want to do what J.C. says and get out of here as soon as possible with my paperwork signed.

I think I need to reframe my life. Maybe I only see the negative because I focus on it, and seeing that personality in an adult like Libby makes me want to never say anything remotely depressing again! How can anything look good to someone who sees everything through dark-colored glasses?

Maybe if I had more Pollyanna attributes, the world would look prettier. It's worth a try. Right, God? God, are you up there? Since I'm in the southern hemisphere, can you hear me better or worse? The Bible says I do not have because I do not ask. Well, I'm asking, Lord.

I want to finish this mission trip well and get my full scholarship, so if you could see it in your heart to put a bug in Claire's ear that this would mean the world to me, I'd be so grateful!

In the late afternoon, we had taken our orders and eaten the slop I made for lunch. It was officially known as chili, but with the absence of meat and beans, it came off as more of a spicy, runny soup. Yum!

I dry the last bowl and place it on the open shelf just as there's a knock at the door. I'm afraid to answer it for fear it's a guy and I'm in the house alone, which will definitely make me a harlot in Libby's eyes. "Heaven knows the guys of Argentina can't stand the temptation that is Daisy Crispin," I say before chastising myself. My positive-speech promise isn't going well.

The person knocks again. Harder this time.

"Who is it?"

"It's Claire! Open up!" She pounds on the door and I lift the latch.

"What are you doing here?"

"I got your message. I'm here to work."

I'm about to blubber, but I don't say a thing. I just grab her up in a bear hug and jump up and down. "I love you, I love you, I love you! God totally answers prayer!"

"Stop. Or I'm going to leave."

"You left the hotel for me?"

"Sure I did. You'd do the same for me. Besides, it's really no fun being pampered when you're all by yourself."

"I'd like to give it a try. I sure hope I'd come rescue you in the same situation."

"You would." Claire has her bobbed hair pinned back with a sparkling barrette, and her makeup is perfect. "But don't hug me like that again. It freaks me out. I like my personal space, you know?"

"Fine. So did you get the part about sleeping in the car?"

"I thought you were kidding."

"I might be, but I'm not sure. Libby is . . . well, she's different," I say. "That dress is cute. Where'd you get it?"

"In town, at this little boutique."

"It's cute," I say again, wistfully.

"I bought it when I was out with your parents last night for dinner."

I'll admit, it's hard to see how easily life comes together for Claire. I know her parents are a mess, but she always looks like she's straight out of a teen style magazine.

"Did you check out of the hotel?" I ask, because she's got only a small leather satchel, no doubt also from one of Recoleta's boutiques. She brought enough luggage to secure passage on a cruise to Europe after this trip.

"I called your parents and told them to come and take the room while I was gone. You should see the dump they're staying in. Your parents sure do love you, Daisy."

"That was so thoughtful! You try to be tough, but I know you're all mushy inside."

"Cut that out! My parents are paying for the room. They'll never know the difference."

I giggle at this. "Well, come on in and see your luxury accommodations. If we're worthy of the house, that is, and not relegated to the car."

"Cool! It's not that loft up there, is it? I always wanted a loft. It's so cool."

"I'll have to sleep on the floor. There's only one cot up there, and again, that's *if* we get to stay in the house. Libby's husband Hank is pretty cool, so I doubt he'll let us sleep in the car."

"Where's the bathroom?"

I pause at this. "It's . . . um, it's outside."

"As in an outhouse! You never said anything about that on the message."

"But there's the loft—so cool, remember? You always wanted one!"

She's not buying it. "Is it clean?"

"I'll clean it for you. Actually, I'll clean for everyone. Apparently, that's one of my duties this week: cleaning the outhouse."

"Gross."

"But here's the good news, and the really awesome part is that you didn't even know this when you came. Okay, the guys working this mission week as translators? They make Max look like a troll."

"Really?" This grabs her interest.

"But we can't really talk to them in front of Libby. She thinks we're all sex-starved teenagers."

"Didn't you tell her about the purity play your parents put on, and that we're the good girls?"

"She's not the type to believe anyone's above temptation. And I gotta admit, wait until you see the vampire, Leo, and you might understand her fears."

"Libby sounds delightful. Wait. What? Vampire?"

"You'll see what I mean. I'm just warning you so you can play it cool. Trust me, it won't be easy."

Claire sweeps her gaze around the room. "I like this place. It's like we get to see Buenos Aires as it really is, not how they portray it to be downtown. I wanted to go home with a real experience like this."

"I guess you got your wish then."

"That's why I was so bummed we never heard anything from Max. What is up with that?"

I shrug. "I haven't the slightest. He was supposed to come back and bring me candy for the kids, and nothing. Well, maybe he implied he'd come back, but he's not one to promise things and not come through. And yet, not a word."

"You have terrible taste in guys."

"Thanks for the support. I'm working on that, you know. Had a bit of an epiphany about it."

"Glad to hear it. You needed one. Some guy calls himself a Christian and you buy it without a shred of evidence."

"I'm trusting."

"You say trusting, I say ignorant."

I do my best to hide my emotions from Claire. The last thing I need is to hear another sermon about the art of being dumped internationally. We all know I could have stayed home for the privilege.

"So what's on the agenda here?" Claire looks around the sparse room again. "I love the way everything is so pieced together and natural. Somehow it's more homey than a designed home where everything is perfect."

I nod. "My house is pieced together."

"But that's more tag sale. This is more authentic."

We both laugh.

"So now we wait for Libby to come back and tell us what to do next, and we try to look really busy," I say.

"Well, look at the cobwebs in that corner. I'll get the broom and take to those."

I look up into the corner and see what Claire's talking about, but I sure never saw it before she said something. She grabs the broom and starts swishing it back and forth on the ceiling. When she can't reach it, she grabs a chair and climbs atop it. The door swings open and Libby stands there taking in the sight.

"Who's this?" Libby, who has to be the palest woman in Argentina, stands with her fists on her hips.

"It—it's—"

"Hey." Claire jumps off the chair with the broom still in her hand and reaches out to shake hands with Libby. "Claire Webster at your service."

A giggle escapes from Libby and she covers her mouth. "Claire? You're here to help?"

She giggled!

"*Sí*," Claire answers. "Here to help you with Vacation Bible School and make sure Daisy goes home with her scholarship. She needs that, you know." Claire says this like she's sharing a dark family secret, but somehow it works.

"We're going to do everything possible to make sure Daisy goes home with her paperwork, and if she's paying attention, she might just learn how to cook while she's here."

"Her parents can't afford to send her to Pepperdine, and that's what she wants."

"Claire!" I lower my brows. "Ixnay!"

"Well, they can't. You know, her dad's disabled. He has his own small business, and it's hard in the Bay Area. Housing prices are sky-high. I mean, even my parents struggle sometimes, and they have my dad's salary. He's a partner in a law firm and does teaching on the side, and my mom inherited money, so they have plenty, but they spend a lot too. I think about some of the stuff she could sell just in her closet and this place could be a palace." Claire seems beyond wordy—even for her.

"You don't say," Libby says. "Come on and sit down. You girls have been working so hard, so let's have some strong coffee. We've earned it. The classroom is all ready for tomorrow."

"She just got here!" I exclaim.

"Daisy, I showed you how to make the coffee this morning, right? The *cafetera* is right there."

"I figured it out," I tell her. "My parents still use a percolator, so it wasn't that difficult."

"Well, start up a carafe and I'll let the boys know we've earned a break. I want us to get to know one another. This is going to be so fun, like one big slumber party this week. I think I have one of the best groups I can remember in past years."

I hide my confusion as I head to the stove, grab the beat-up aluminum *cafetera*, and fill it to capacity with generous amounts of ground coffee. I put the teakettle on to boil the water and wait. The whole time Libby and Claire are talking and laughing like they're old friends, and I'm feeling like I'm in another dimension. As if *Inception* has come to life and I'm left to make heads or tails of my world.

"So, Claire, what type of help can you offer me this week? Do you like to cook?"

"Heavens no!" She laughs.

"Claire's an actress. Maybe she could play one of the parts?" I offer.

"Oh, I was going to be Queen Esther, and I wondered how I'd ever get the kids to believe in her beauty." Libby laughs. "Do you think you could read the lines in Spanish?"

"I can have them memorized by morning."

"Oh my!" Libby claps her hands. "Did you hear that, Daisy? I have my Queen Esther!"

I try not to be offended that she never thought of me to play the heroine queen, but I take to the coffeepot with a new vengeance. I stare at the two of them, who seem to have become fast friends in a matter of minutes, and I seriously wonder if I'm cursed. Maybe there's something hanging over the generations of my family members that I know nothing about. Maybe no matter how hard I try, I will be thwarted in everything in which I try to better myself. This does not bode well for my power-of-positive-thinking prayer.

"I know, right?" Claire says in response to something Libby said, and they both break into laughter, while I'm the third wheel.

There's a knock at the door.

"Can you get that, Daisy?" Libby asks. "We're talking."

"Sure, no problem." I open the door and the guys are all standing there in their boy-band perfection. I am totally waiting for them to break into song. I look back at Claire and see her reaction to the guys, and there it is! I want to say to her, *I know, right?* But I can hardly do that with Libby thinking the guys are all ready to sweep us off our feet with Latino flair.

"Is that coffee we smell?" Leo, aka Vampire Boy, says.

I open the door wider. "Yes, come on in."

"What else smells so good?" Jose asks.

"It's dinner. I found a recipe for the pork bones the neighbor brought over. I added some beans and rice and seasoned it with chopped onions and garlic, and you know, I think it's going to be really filling."

"You did that yourself?" Claire gets up and looks into the pot. "It smells really good, Daisy."

"I know, huh?"

Jose puts his chin on my shoulder and looks over into the pot. "Daisy, I think I might have to marry you."

Libby laughs at this, and if I didn't know better I'd think Claire was serving as some kind of magical pixie dust in the room. I watch as she continues to stare at the guys and takes in Leo's eyes.

"Claire," Libby says, "this is our team for the next week. Oscar is the tall one there, Jose is the one with the curly hair, and Leo is the one Daisy calls a vampire because of his blue eyes. J.C., the only blond, isn't here right now. He is the one who will be going to Pepperdine with Daisy. He's from Arizona. Gentlemen, this is Claire."

"Hey, guys." Claire goes right back to talking with Libby as if the guys don't exist, and I'm wondering if her acting skills have gotten better or if she's just not into the whole Latino thing.

"Where's J.C.?" I ask the guys. "Claire, J.C. received the same scholarship I did, so he's doing the same mission trip. Isn't that cool? I'll have a friend at Pepperdine before I get there."

"We haven't seen J.C.," Oscar says as he looks at the others.

"He wasn't in the classroom with you?"

"I haven't seen him since lunch," Oscar answers. "Did you see him, Jose?"

Jose shakes his head. "He was going to walk that toddler home who came with the bottle. That was the last time I saw him."

Something in the pit of my stomach feels off, and I decide

I'd better look for J.C. "Claire, can you take over the coffee? I'm going to go see if he's in one of the outbuildings."

Claire looks at me like I've grown another head. "I don't know how to make coffee. I just order what I want at Starbucks."

"Leo, you go look for J.C.," Libby orders.

"I'll go!" I grab my shoes before Libby has a chance to protest. I turn the heat off the soup and cover it.

"I'll go too," Leo says. "It's getting late."

"Did you see which way he went? Didn't you think to ask where he was going?"

"Because he is a . . . how you say—big boy?"

"J.C.!" I yell once we get outside. I cup my hands around my mouth. "J.C., are you out here?" Little kids scatter at my voice, and I look at the cracked earth and wonder how these kids make it in this environment. The rains have just come, but the earth is already dry and parched and it's the middle of winter. "It's a harsh life down here."

"You have no idea. But the kids are so excited. They've been hanging around all day. The one J.C. took home couldn't have been more than two, and he came in just a diaper with a bottle in his hand."

"J.C.!" I yell again, and a little boy comes out from behind one of the scrappy buildings. He has wide brown eyes and his head is shaved, no doubt to ward off the lice that can find him in the outskirts of the city. I scratch my head unwittingly. "*Tú veo amigo*?"

"Your Spanish is terrible," Leo says.

"Hence the reason for an interpreter. You ask him."

Leo rambles something off that sounds like gibberish, and the boy answers him in just as quick a manner. I realize why I don't speak another language.

"*Gracias*," Leo says. He begins to run and I follow. He takes out his cell phone and hands it to me. "Dial 107! Tell them to come to the mission. Tell them the canal!" With that, Leo runs ahead of me, and I'm left grappling with the cell phone. I follow after him while I dial.

"*Emergencia*," the voice answers.

I try with English, and she answers me back. "Oh, praise God, you speak English." I tell her about the mission and the canals.

"*Sistema de Canales*?" she asks, and I realize with horror that she wasn't speaking English.

"*Sí*," I answer, praying I've told her correctly while my legs carry me farther without thought. "Yes!"

"*Emergencia*?" The woman is rambling faster than I can understand, but I know she's asking me if there's an emergency.

"*Yo no se*," I tell her honestly. "I don't know. Just come." What was the word for *come*? I couldn't remember to save my life. Or someone else's, for that matter.

"*Hay alguien en el canal?*"

"Is someone in the canal?" I repeat with joy at my understanding.

"*Sí.*"

"*Yo no se.*" I'm working in the kitchen! *La cocina*! If we had a food emergency, I'd be fine. I think with annoyance at how little the phrases of high school Spanish are helping me.

My heart is pounding a mile a minute as I race to keep up with Leo, who runs to what seems to be the end of the earth and then halts abruptly. He holds his arm out to let me know not to go any farther. I hear him call J.C.'s name again, and this time I hear J.C. answer.

"Thank you, Jesus!"

I catch up with Leo and he stops me. In the middle of this seemingly desert environment, there's an aqueduct made of cement. Clearly this country has few lawyers because there's no fence and not a protective sign in sight. Just a crevice that opens up in the middle of the dirt expanse.

I can't imagine how the kids in the town have been protected from this danger. I look down and see little water, no more than a trickle. J.C. is perched up against one of the cement walls, but he's slouched over and appears weak as he looks up at Leo and me.

"Are you alone?" Leo asks him.

"Yes, I was on my way back. The baby's home safe." His voice sounds hoarse.

"Are you hurt?"

J.C. nods, and in his nervousness he breaks into Spanish. "*Escorpión. Tenaza!*"

I look at Leo's dangerous blue eyes.

"He got stung by a scorpion." He looks back down into the canal where a steady stream of water is splashing J.C. "Before or after you fell?"

"After."

"Can you walk?"

"I stumbled after I got stung. I may have broken my arm, and my ankle's twisted."

"What do we do?" I ask.

"You called 107?"

"They're still on the line." I hand the phone to Leo and he rambles, waits, and rambles some more.

"They're on their way, J.C.," Leo says. "I gave them better directions to our location. We have to try to get you out of the canal. The water can rush through at any time, and if your arm is broken, you won't be able to swim."

This is terrible. "Can I get you something to make you more comfortable?" I ask.

He shakes his downturned head, and I find myself wishing for a look at his gray-green eyes.

"Run back to the house and tell Libby. See if she has any antivenom there, and find a rope if you can." Leo stares back at J.C., who is at least twelve feet down.

"Will he be all right?"

Leo ignores me. "Have you had your tetanus?" he asks J.C.

J.C. nods slowly.

"Daisy, go back to the house now!"

"Will he be okay?"

Leo's eyes turn dark. "The antivenom. Run!"

I run back to the house as fast as my legs will carry me, praying out loud the whole time. My breath is labored, but I keep shouting to God, afraid for J.C.'s life. God wouldn't take someone like this. J.C. only came to help.

I can barely speak as I strike open the door. "J.C. Canal. Scorpion. Antivenom!" I manage through my struggling breath.

"Oh my goodness! Scorpions aren't out in the day!" Libby shouts and throws back her chair as she gets out of it. "The antivenom is in the classroom!" She runs outside, and I follow her to the building, where she opens a locked cabinet with a key she wears on her wrist. "I have to lock everything or it will be stolen and sold," she explains. "How long ago was he stung?"

"I don't know," I tell her. "I need a rope too. He's in the canal."

"Did you call 107?"

"I did. They're on their way."

"It has to be administered within four hours, but the sooner the better."

"He's been gone all afternoon." My anxiety can't be hidden. "He sounded weak, and I think his arm is broken too, so he's in a lot of pain."

Libby's expression warms and she rubs my shoulder. "He'll be fine, Daisy. The sting isn't that dangerous to him. He's an adult. I'm more concerned about getting him out of that canal before any water comes. Just calm down or you'll be of no use to anyone. The antivenom is only a precaution. Give him the shot somewhere above his heart, maybe in his arm. Not the broken one."

"No, not me." I step back.

"You have to go, I don't know where he is exactly. You'll get there faster." She opens another cabinet and pulls out a tired-looking rope. "Give him this cold pack to place on the sting and see if you can't find the scorpion for the medics."

I shake my head again.

"Go, Daisy!" She pushes a bag of stuff at me. "Make a paste of the baking soda after you've given the shot. The shot first! Then bring him back to the house if you can get him up."

"But his arm . . ."

"Then wait for the medics." Libby's voice gets low. "Daisy. You're fine. You're doing fine."

I nod and she pushes me out the door. I run, whispering a mantra to myself. "I can do this."

As I get to the edge of the canal, there's no sign of Leo, and I look down to see him in the canal next to J.C. Leo has taken off his shirt and wrapped J.C.'s arm in it.

"I've got the antivenom!"

"Throw it down!" he yells. I hear a siren wailing in the distance.

"I think help is coming. There's a cold pack in there. Smack it and it will turn cold. Put it on the stinger site. Do you see the scorpion?"

"It stung me up there and I jumped," J.C. says. "That's how I ended up down here."

Immediately I start doing the Mexican hat dance and look around my feet, but I don't see any sign of the monster.

"You need to wear shoes out here. These kind come out in the wet weather, but usually not during the day," Leo says. "J.C. just got lucky."

"Give him the shot above the heart!"

Leo nods, but he's already done the deed. J.C. doesn't look any the worse for wear, yet I still can't help but dread the upcoming week. I want everything to go perfectly, but my head can't help getting in the way of optimism.

I look down at my flip-flopped feet and feel as if I've got creepy-crawlies all over my body. I start to pray, *Lord forgive me for not getting on my knees, but the last thing we need is another scorpion sting. Please let J.C. be all right, and Lord, make the days here pass like a brisk wind. Amen.*

J.C. stares up at me from under his shaggy mop of blond hair, and he grins with his Hollywood style, as if he's comforting me and wants me to stop worrying. I may not know my place here yet in Argentina, but I know that grin finally made me feel like I belong here.

8

Into the evening, the commotion has died down, the dishes from supper are washed, and we all sit around the table trying to find our bearings without Leo and J.C. Leo accompanied J.C. to the medical clinic just as a precaution, and there's a definite tension left hanging in the air.

"Your pork stew was tasty," Hank says to me. "You keep this up and we may have to keep you, and you can forget college."

I smile. "It was just reading directions."

"We have to work out the sleeping arrangements for tonight," Libby says.

"The girls will sleep in the other loft, and you and I will sleep in our room and pull the curtain," Hank says. "It's only for a week. If they can sacrifice, so can we."

Libby doesn't say another word and it's apparently been decided.

"I think we'll have to have J.C. in here in the living room. Not sure he should be out in the classroom with a broken arm. Too many things he could fall on," Hank says.

"I can't have him in here with the girls."

"You'll be right there. What could possibly happen?"

She doesn't have an answer for this. She rises and pours herself another cup of coffee.

"We'll need the snacks ready for the kids at 9:30 sharp for the first group. It's ants on a log. You just put peanut butter—not too much—on three inches of celery and then three raisins."

I nod.

"Hank, what about J.C. tomorrow? You can't leave him in here all day. Daisy will be in here cooking. I've left her a full day's agenda."

"Then she'll be too busy to make a pass at the invalid," Hank says plainly, and the rest of the guys laugh at this.

Libby purses her lips.

"J.C. isn't Daisy's type. You don't have a thing to worry about," Claire says. "She has this thing about being loyal to doofuses until the day she dies. Too much poet in her blood, I think."

"It seems we're shorthanded again, but I suppose the Lord will have to provide. Maybe one of the local girls can help Daisy in the kitchen." Libby walks back to the table.

"I'll help where I can in between Queen Esther's role," Claire says, and Libby smiles and pats her on the cheek.

"You're a kind girl, Claire. I'm so excited for you all to meet the children tomorrow. They will steal your hearts and change your lives."

My stomach finally unclenches for the first time since I've been in Libby's presence. It does me good to hear her talk so warmly about the children, and it gives me unprecedented hope that I'll get through the next week.

"Boys," Libby continues, "there are extra cots in the back outbuilding. I think you should take them and shake them out and use them. It will be more trouble in the morning to clean them up, but if the scorpions are out, it's better not to be on the cement floor. Here's the key to the outbuilding." She hands it over.

Jose shakes his curly hair. "That gives me the willies."

Oscar nods in agreement.

"I've never seen a scorpion out there. But think of the children. They often don't have the luxury of a cot. One year we did a fund-raiser to buy more, but often the parents take them for themselves." Libby stares at her espadrille-clad feet.

I watch Claire shudder and lift her feet ever so slightly off the cement floor.

"We can't let J.C.'s crisis interfere with all we have to do. Boys, you get out in the classroom and finish up, and Daisy will start preparing J.C.'s cot. Daisy, face it toward the door so he's not looking up into the lofts, if you will."

I nod.

Libby walks toward me, looks me up and down, and sighs. "You've certainly changed the way we do things around here this week."

Oscar and Jose pick up their coffee mugs, bring them to the sink, and walk out without a word.

"I expected the Latino culture to be more talkative—you know, social," I whisper to Claire.

"Daisy, quit that whispering!" Libby shouts. "Go out and get one of those extra cots before Jose locks the building. J.C. should be back soon. They'll probably have him on steroids or antibiotics." Libby clicks her tongue in an annoyed way. "I just hope we haven't lost another pair of hands. Hank, is there anyone down at the plant we can borrow? I think I've got everyone from the church that can spare the week."

Hank shakes his head. "You've got everyone, as far as I know. We'll be fine. You always worry and it always works out. It's time for some of that faith you're so famous for."

"If Claire and I are going to be in here cooking, I can look after J.C.'s medications," I say. "As long as you can trust us."

Libby's mouth flattens. "Yes, that would be beneficial if I didn't have to worry about J.C. in here all day. Are you two sure you can handle it? I can call Claire when it's time for her to play Esther."

"Is there a menu for what we're supposed to make?" Claire asks.

"Everything is on the chart there for the weekly schedule. Daisy seems to be finding her way around the kitchen very quickly." Libby glares at me. "You're a quick study, Daisy. I may have been wrong about you." Then she turns toward her beloved. "Claire, I'm so happy you've joined us. It takes a very special girl to give up her free time and come to a foreign country not to vacation"—Libby glowers at me—"but to go where they're needed when called upon."

"I called her!" I hear myself say, but with that, I decide suddenly that it's unhealthy to force someone into liking me. Libby has the choice of not liking me, and I'm not going to keep hiking up the same tree only to fall out of it and wonder how I got there. Libby . . . Chase . . . Max. It's a pattern with me. If people don't like me, I try harder instead of just understanding that not everyone is going to like me and moving on to people who do. Like Claire.

"I'll go get the cot."

The door is wide open, and I see the guys at the outbuilding across the cracked, parched dirt field that has probably seen its share of pickup soccer games. I wonder about these children milling around in anticipation for the biggest event the small village has going on—I wonder if any of them will get to go to college. I wonder if my financial degree might make any difference in their life. In mine . . .

"You all right?" Oscar asks. He scratches his upper lip.

"Yeah, I'm fine. I need to get a cot for J.C. Libby is going to set him up in the house."

"She's not worried you'll pounce on him?" Jose laughs.

"I guess I've earned her trust. Either that or she gives J.C. more credit."

Jose gets a cot down from an old wooden shelf in the shed and dusts it off. "J.C. would be a fool if he didn't take the opportunity to plant one on you while he's in there."

"Very funny."

"I'm not joking. He's not in your league, though. I think you need that Latino thing going on. Do you tango?"

"Badly."

"Didn't you tango in town with some of the experts on the street?"

"Didn't have time. We dropped Claire at the hotel and came straight here."

Jose tucks the cot under his arm. "I'll take it in for you. Daisy, you really don't look so good. Are you sure you're okay?"

"Jose, why do you think Libby dislikes me so much?"

Jose looks at the house, then back at me. He shrugs. "Does she like anybody?" He puts the cot down and places a hand on my shoulder. "Do you know what I think it is?"

"What?"

"I think you can tell who likes you and who doesn't. Most of us don't pay that close attention."

"Yeah," I say absently. "Maybe that's it. I just thought people should get to know you before they don't like you. I'm very likable."

He laughs. "Of course you are. And Libby is very unlikable. So maybe it's a compliment."

"It's not." I shake my head.

A car pulls up in the yard, and I expect to see J.C. and Leo in Hank's boat of a car, but it's Max in a blue compact. My heart starts to pound, and I'm angry at it for betraying what I feel at the sight of flaky Max.

"Who's that? Local volunteer?"

"That's Max. I knew him in California."

"Ah," Jose says. "I'll get the cot in the house."

"I'll be in the classroom setting up camp for the night," Oscar says.

Suddenly I'm alone, waiting . . . as Max walks the seemingly endless expanse of dirt between us.

"Hi."

"Where have you been?"

"I got tied up at work. I couldn't make it back out here last night. How's it going?"

"Fine." I shrug. "Did you get me the candy?"

"Oh." He slaps his forehead. "I totally forgot. But I have your money." He digs into his back pocket.

"Forget it. There's nothing I can do with it here."

"No, I want to give it back to you before I forget." He hands me a few crumpled American dollars. "You're mad at me. I let you down."

"No. I'm mad at myself. I don't think I trust the right people, and it's made life more complicated than it needs to be. I want to be drama-free."

"Is that possible with Claire in your life?"

"Drama-free with the exception of my best friend's drama."

"Where does that leave me?"

"Max, why are you here?"

"I was able to get away from work."

"I don't even know what kind of work you do."

"You never asked."

"I'm asking now."

"I drive a bus for an old-age home. Take them to the pharmacy, doctor's appointments. That kind of thing."

"They didn't have any candy at the pharmacy?"

"What do you want from me, Daisy? I can't drive the bus here."

"I guess I want answers, Max." I hate how shrewish I sound, but my words keep coming. "I don't want you to be shrouded in mystery, and if you are, then I guess I don't want the drama in my life."

He nods curtly. "Fine."

"That's all you have to say?"

"My mom is sick, Daisy. I'm working to take care of her, and I come home at night and have to see to her needs. It's not like I'm out partying. I thought you knew me well enough to give me the benefit of the doubt."

"Max, I'm sorry. I didn't know. Why didn't you tell me that?"

"I don't know." He holds a palm up. "You're right. Drama sucks. I should have told you, but I thought you had enough to worry about down here, so I didn't. I'll see ya." He twists in the dirt and walks toward his car.

He'll see me? When? I'm compelled to go after him, but something stops me in my tracks—like a physical pressure. Soon the feeling passes, and I walk toward the main house thinking sometimes this is all the closure one is ever going to get. He never even told me what was wrong with his mother, so how close were we anyway?

"That's so true!" Libby is saying to Claire as I walk inside the rickety structure. "I do wonder what J.C. was doing down by the canal in the first place. I suppose I should have warned you all it was there. Daisy, come on over here, I'm about to show you how to feed an army on a dime."

I walk over to the kitchen and see a pot full of pinto beans soaking.

"These have been soaking all night so that they won't cause . . . well, it's just the way we prepare them. We soak them all night, and then the next day we cook them, wash the pot, and soak the next batch of beans."

I nod.

"Was that Max out there?" Claire asks.

"Yeah. It's over."

"Did it ever start?"

"I guess not. I'm done with guys."

"So soon?" Libby asks.

"I have a terrible record. Libby, will the beans crack while they're soaking?"

Let's face it, flatulence is the perfect discussion when avoiding the subject of my love life. I'm paying special attention to the cooking lessons because obviously my love life is going nowhere quick, so I might as well hone my skills.

"Her selector is off. She needs someone else to pick for her," Claire says matter-of-factly.

"I'd pick that J.C. for her. He may not be too bright, but he's a cute thing. He must be book smart too if he got into that Pepperdine of hers."

"J.C. is out of my league, Libby, and besides, I thought your whole deal was making sure no one mingled with the opposite sex on your property."

"Oh, I'd kick you both out, don't get me wrong. I'm only saying I think you two would be darling together. You could bring the common sense to his book smart ways, and you two would be unstoppable."

Claire laughs at this. But I hardly think jokes at my expense are funny at the moment.

9

My Life: Stop—July 8

Factoid: 329 million people are native Spanish speakers. I am not one of them, and never was this more apparent than today.

It's the first day of Vacation Bible School and the compound is abuzz already. I suppose I shouldn't say "compound," as that implies cult or underground military chamber . . . but then again, Libby does have a few things in common with certain military leaders and cult organizers. Of course, it's not politically correct to say that. It's just true.

The pace is frenetic and exciting, and there's a lot less English going on around here than there has been, so I am feeling more lost than usual. I've had three years of high school Spanish, but with the speed natives speak it, I catch about every sixth word—which leaves a lot to be desired in the area of overall comprehension. No one has time to speak in an alternative language (mine!), so there's a bit of Spanglish going on as well. I'm better at that.

J.C. is back, and he's sleeping soundly in the middle of the living room. I suppose because he looks half dead, Libby feels it's safe to leave him with me—that I won't pounce on him. Sigh. What is up with that?

We all had a breakfast of scrambled eggs with hot sauce alongside J.C. in bed. I guess Libby doesn't want him to get too comfortable with being sick when she's got work to do. I thought for sure those gorgeous eyes would pop open at the scent of the pepper sauce, if not the noise of clanking silverware, but J.C. slept through it all. As soon as Libby and the rest left the main house, I actually checked J.C.'s breathing. I did so in speed mode so Libby didn't come in and catch me and accuse me of making a pass at Sleeping Beauty.

But I'm done with guys. Even if Libby would never believe that. Hey, Claire probably wouldn't believe it either, but it's time I stopped wasting energy on romance and focused on my education. Clearly God doesn't think I'm cut out for both.

In a way, I feel invigorated at the idea of having my love life behind me and well into the future. I'm too young to think of such things anyway, right? It saves my tender heart from being broken again. I made it through high *school without a steady boyfriend. Surely I can manage college as a loser as well—it's a lot easier to get lost in the crowd there, and no one needs to know I'm dateless. I mean, a single girl. Nothing wrong with being single! Guys do it all the time, and it has this free and fabulous connotation. It's time we girls changed that for ourselves.*

Maybe I'm entering new territory, like a purity pioneer, if you will. Although with Libby the man-hater married—and to a really decent guy—it's doing nothing to swell myself with pride.

I washed up the breakfast dishes, and now I'm sitting on the sofa watching J.C.'s expansive chest rise and fall with each breath and being thankful I'm over guys and dating. Though I have to tell God, it would be a lot easier to get totally over them if J.C. looked like a hairy troll rather than a blond cherub with gorgeous gray-green eyes.

I should start fixing lunch and finishing the morning snack. I just can't help but hope my travel journal will have SOME form of travel in it before I'm done here. Some form of travel other than climbing up and down the ladder to my pathetically hard spot beside the cot.

Libby storms through the door. "Today's the day!"

I shut my journal and stuff it under the couch. She has renewed vigor and purpose at seeing all the kids outside, and she is not happy to find me on the sofa.

"Loafing already? Daisy, come on, you've got work to do. All this celery needs to be cut and the ants on a log made. Come on, snap, snap!" She shakes J.C. awake with both of her mitts. "How are you feeling?" she asks him in a tone that's loud enough for the entire camp to hear.

J.C. groans from under his blanket.

"I see you're still not up to par. I need to move you. Daisy needs the prep space."

Libby lifts up the foot-end of J.C.'s cot and roughly slides him across the room with the cot legs squealing, until he's farther from the kitchen and closer to the fireplace—which I still have yet to see used. Staying with Libby is like living in a cold, concrete cave.

"Now you won't have to get out of bed until you're ready," she says as though she's done him a favor. "But when you're ready, we'll obviously need to move you so we can run the camp more efficiently. How does the sting site feel?"

"It's my arm." He moans. "It's throbbing. The sting site isn't that bad. Just ugly." He uncovers his foot from the blanket and shows us a red volcano of pain near his toes.

I cringe just looking at it, but Libby is still matter-of-fact in tone. "Oh my, that's a good one. Must have been a baby scorpion. They'll put a hard cast on your arm as soon as the swelling goes down. Are you keeping up on your pain meds?" She shouts to me, "Daisy, come get J.C. more of his pain meds and get the potatoes going for lunch before you start the celery. He doesn't need to take that on an empty stomach." Libby sits alongside J.C. on his cot. "Daisy's going to take care of you today. I assume you're making arrangements to get home, no?"

"No, I can get up and help. I don't want to be a burden."

"Don't be silly. You can't leave while your arm is still throbbing. It should stop throbbing by tomorrow morning." Libby pats his leg a bit too hard and J.C. flinches. "Hank was right. We had extra volunteers show up from church at the last minute. God is so good. If you do plan to stay, you can just help with more of the cleanup at the end to get your college credit, but the swelling won't go down at all if you're up and about, so I'd say stay down for now. I'm certain Hank has some yard work that needs to be done at the end of the week. He talked about building a pergola." Libby has a smile on her face, and for all intents and purposes, she apparently thinks she's being gracious. "Daisy, I'm going to get things started outside. The children are so excited. Here we go!"

Libby leaves the room, and J.C. and I both breathe a sigh of relief.

I walk across the room to the kitchen. Claire and I shredded potatoes until late into the night so I'd be ready for lunch and still able to prep the celery stick snacks. We covered them with a tiny bit of lemon juice to keep them from turning brown, and now they'll provide a filling meal for the kids—maybe the only one they'll get today, which still makes me want to cry every time I think about it. It almost seems laughable that I complained about homemade clothes when half these kids don't even have shoes. For all Libby's faults, I can see she does love the children and want to see them well fed with both the Word of God and food.

I open the icebox, take the shredded potatoes out, and rummage for some orange juice so that J.C. can take his medications. I fill up a glass and hand him the pills, then help him drink from the glass.

He groans from the movement. “I can’t be sick here. You heard her. Now she’s not going to sign off on my scholarship.”

“I don’t think you’re in a position to worry about that, and I think an insurance agency offering a scholarship knows enough about injury that you should be excused. Besides, maybe Libby says all that to keep us on our toes.”

We both look at one another and say, “Nah!”

“When these meds kick in, I’ll get up and help you with snacks and lunch.”

“Why don’t you just stay in bed and I’ll say that you helped? I think we’d both feel better that way.”

“Lie? To fulfill a mission?”

“Abraham lied about Sarah being his wife in the Bible.”

“I don’t think it’s a how-to section, though.”

J.C. makes me laugh. “No. Do you want some eggs? I’ll make them fresh. The other ones are hard by now, and you slept through breakfast.”

“It’s the pain meds. They make me tired. But I’ll take the hard ones. The last thing you need is more work. Isn’t Claire going to help you in the kitchen?”

“She’s playing Queen Esther. She’ll be back.”

“Did your friend show up with the candy finally?” he asks, and I’m honored he remembered about Max.

“He showed up. But not with the candy. I do believe he dumped me. Or I dumped him because I didn’t believe in him enough, and that was his excuse. I don’t know. Something happened. Maybe it was lost in translation.”

“Or I was right. He’s a jerk and he wants you to believe it’s you. I’m telling you, I’ve seen it time and time again. You girls will take on the guilt as easily as you’ll wear a new outfit.”

I smile at him. "You're not too kind to your own gender."

"It comes from having a psychologist mother. She sets me straight on the games people play. Like you girls pretending to be helpless for male attention."

"Maybe that's been my problem all along. I'm not that helpless. Do you think it would help me if I acted weak and needy?" I lift the back of my hand to my forehead and say with a Southern accent, "Oh, if I could only lift all these potatoes, but alas, I am so very weak and hope a big, strong man will come around to help me so I can get lunch ready on time."

"Oh brother."

"No? It doesn't work for me?"

"It might help you find another loser."

We're both laughing when the tiny boy from yesterday toddles into the house. He's still wearing only a diaper and holding his bottle, which is filthy with handprints.

"Oh, sweetheart. Aren't you cold?" I take my sweatshirt off and put it on the boy, and he grins and waddles precariously over to J.C.

The boy points to J.C.'s arm. "Owie?"

"*Sí*," J.C. tells him. "Owie."

The little boy is filthy and barefoot, though his diaper appears fresh.

"Do you think I could give him a bath? I can get warm water in the sink."

J.C. shakes his head. "That might tick Libby off. You don't have clean clothes for him anyway. Unless Libby has something out in the classroom we don't know about."

"Libby must have some out in the classroom. I could check."

"I don't know, Daisy. I don't think you better mess with it."

"He's just a baby."

"I know, but I heard his stepfather yesterday when I took him home, and he's not a nice man. You don't want to get Libby into any trouble, and something tells me that's exactly what would happen."

I look at the dirty little boy with his pudgy cheeks and shaved head, his swollen stomach. The last thing I want to do is cause trouble, but this child is so darling and I want someone to care for him.

"Just take him out to the classroom." J.C. stands and sways a bit to find his balance. "Never mind, you've got work to do. I'll take him."

"No, I've got this. Just relax. You need to let the swelling go down on both your arm and your foot. You're like a walking balloon. Your foot is twice its size. Sit down."

J.C. grabs the toddler, and his expression changes. "Daisy, look." He swings the boy up into his good arm and shows me a distinct black-and-blue bruise on the boy's hindquarters. "He couldn't have fallen here."

"People are allowed to spank their kids, though, right?" I say tentatively, though I can't imagine what such a small boy could have done to deserve such a spanking.

"This is a toddler. Look at the size of his welt." The boy squirms in J.C.'s arms as he tries to show me the bruise's topography, and I slather some peanut butter on a celery stalk and hold it out to the boy, who takes it readily.

"We have to tell Libby. She'll know what we can do and how the law works."

"I don't know, Daisy. Libby is swamped today, and she's not going to like us meddling in the neighborhood's business. What if she tells us to do nothing? Then we have to listen to her if we want our papers signed, and I'm not sure I could live with myself under those circumstances."

"But she might tell us exactly what to do. Maybe we can call the police and ask them what we might do."

J.C. speaks to the little boy. "Pablo, *alguien hacerle daño a usted?* Did someone hurt you?"

He shakes his head.

"Pablo," J.C. says again, and the little boy curls up into J.C.'s neck.

"No casa."

"You don't want to go home?"

"*No casa*," the toddler says again.

"J.C., we have to tell Libby." My stomach is sick at the thought, but there's a way things are done down here, and we just don't know enough.

"Libby knows the man, Daisy. She has to, and as much as this little guy has been around the house in the last few days, you can't tell me she doesn't have an idea what's going on."

"If she sees the bruise—listen, I'm no Libby fan, but I can't believe she'd turn her back on a child. I'm not willing to believe it."

"I tried to tell her that the house looked badly cared for, but she told me already I didn't understand how people down here lived and to just do as I was told and mind my own business." J.C.'s gray-green eyes look right through me. "If we're wrong, the police will work it out. If we're not, we leave Pablo to fend for himself."

I look at the toddler again and bite my bottom lip. I know J.C. is right, but the consequences . . . "Libby could revoke our paperwork."

"She could, but don't you think the insurance company

would understand if we did the right thing? We've got the power of numbers anyway. It's our word against hers."

"Yes, if we did the right thing, but what if we're jumping to conclusions? What if he fell like you did yesterday, and we're causing trouble where there isn't any?"

"Pablo, *tu papá te golpearon*?" J.C. asks if Pablo's father hit him.

"*Sí*," Pablo says and curls up against J.C.'s chest. J.C. has him snuggled in his good arm, and the sight is heartwarming.

"Let me take him before your good arm wears out." I reach out to the boy, and he comes readily and snuggles into the crook of my neck. "Oh my, he's such a little monkey. I love him."

J.C. sticks his wallet into his back pocket. "I'm taking him to the medical clinic. I know where it is from yesterday. You'd better stay here in case Libby comes looking for me."

"J.C., you can't drive."

"My rental car is right outside," he says, missing my point.

"Your foot is twice its natural size. You have a broken arm. That can't be safe. You don't want Pablo hurt any more, do you? You'd feel terrible."

"Have you ever driven in Argentina?" he asks.

"No, but you stay here and I'll drive him. Tell me how to get there. As long as I don't have to go on the main freeway, I'll be fine. I drive in Silicon Valley. It can't be any worse here."

"No, you won't drive. We don't even know if they'll do anything, and then we'd have to sneak back here."

"I think we should ask Libby," I tell him as I pull Pablo closer to me.

"Ask her." J.C. holds his good arm open. "Be my guest."

"I'll do it." I set Pablo on the sofa and march outside, then look behind me to see if he's watching. He is standing in the doorway, so I head to the classroom.

The small room is filled with children ranging in age from mere preschoolers to maybe junior high. I find Libby in the crowd and walk toward her. She holds her hand up to halt me. I draw in a deep breath.

"Did you finish the snacks?" she asks.

"Nearly."

"Lunch?"

"It's on the stove."

"J.C.'s all right?"

"Yes. I just wondered, is it legal in Argentina to—"

"Pablo!" I hear a deep, gruff voice outside and my heart starts to pound.

"Oh, that man. He's back again!" Libby hikes her cotton skirt up around her boots and heads outside. I follow her and see what I'd describe in America as a star criminal suspect on *Cops*. He's unshaven, wearing a wife-beater shirt, and his hands are rolled into fists, which makes him look like a gorilla of a man. Libby walks toward him in the same stance.

Libby speaks in Spanish, but it's slow and methodical enough that I can understand her. "I told you, Pablo isn't here. You don't want him signed up, I didn't sign him up. Get off my property."

"You got my boy!" he accuses in English.

"Go inside and look if you don't believe me, but if you scare any of those children in there, I'll have the police out here immediately and make you get off my land."

The man looks into the room and scans it, practically foaming at the mouth with anger. "If Gloria comes home and finds that boy missing . . ."

"If I see him, I'll send him home, but he's not here. Had someone bring him home yesterday, then he got stung by a scorpion on the way back. In the middle of the day."

The man yells curses in Spanish as he stomps away from the house. Libby turns and hisses under her breath, "Animal!"

"Does he want to hurt the boy?" I ask Libby.

"I wouldn't put it past him, but the boy runs off all the time. Can't stand to be around him, I suppose. The mother is off working most of the day and he's her only child, so there's no one but that lug to keep an eye on him. He gets to the drink and the child disappears."

"But do you think he would hurt him?"

"I have no idea, but he's a frustrated man, and that can't be a good sign. He sure wants to blame everyone else when the boy goes missing. But why do you keep asking?"

"I would want to hide the boy, naturally, if he was hurt. Wouldn't you?"

"Daisy, if I tried to take on every parent around here who spanked their child, I'd have no trust at all in the village. This is the way to get them to God."

"But surely safety—"

"Do you know where Pablo is, Daisy? You seem awfully curious about this subject."

"I—"

Libby rushes into the house and I run after her, grasping my throat. I must not be meant for the missionary lifestyle because I can't see the bigger picture if someone is hurting that little boy.

10

Libby enters the house as though she's on the same rampage as Pablo's stepfather. I enter behind her and see J.C. in bed, looking innocent in every way. He stares up at the two of us. "Daisy, thank goodness you're here. Can you grab my pain pills? I thought you weren't coming back. I should have taken two this morning when you gave me one."

"Did you call your grandmother yet to change your flight?" Libby asks him.

J.C. nods. "I did. I texted her. I'll be working at the food bank when I get home to fulfill my requirements, so you don't need to worry about me. She's already worked it out with the insurance company. I'm sorry I wasn't more helpful."

"Very good," Libby says without the benefit of compassion, and I'm seriously disliking her at the moment. Not that she was ever my greatest aspiration in terms of people.

"You're making him go home? I thought he planned to stay through the week."

"He's of no use to me like that, set up in the middle of my kitchen, is he? I thought you said the snacks were almost done. Where are they?"

"They're in the fridge on trays. But J.C.'s hurt. He got hurt helping a little boy who needed to find his way home."

"Pablo could find his way home from downtown Buenos Aires."

"Why does he keep running away from home? He's just a baby."

Libby narrows her eyes. "How do you know how old he is?"

"Uh, J.C. told me he carried him home. I assumed he was tiny. Plus he was here yesterday morning." I try to remember if Pablo had been here any other time, but I can't. Libby doesn't seem to be looking for trouble, though, so I'm safe.

"Don't worry about Pablo, you've got enough worries with getting all those snacks done in time."

"They're done," I say proudly. "Just a few raisins to plop on."

She eyes me suspiciously and then shuts the door, leaving J.C. and me alone.

"Do you think she trusts us now? She shut the door."

"Wait for it." He stays immobile in bed, and the door thrusts open again.

"Did you forget something?" I ask Libby.

She shakes her head. "Fifteen minutes. No later on the snacks."

I nod. She leaves the door open this time and heads back to the classroom.

"She hates me."

"*No me gusta Señora Libby.*" Pablo crawls out of J.C.'s bed.

"Are you nuts? We're the ones who are going to get accused of child abuse."

"Just cover for me."

"You're not driving like that! For one thing, you're on pain meds that could choke a horse. You are not driving anywhere in your condition."

"You can't come with me. She's itching for an excuse to send you back home without your scholarship paperwork, and I'm not sending this kid home again. Not without some answers first."

I look at Pablo's forlorn face and my mission becomes clear. "I couldn't live with myself if I didn't get him checked out. But something tells me I'm going to regret this."

J.C. smiles. "That's my girl." He bends down to Pablo's level and tells him to hide in the cabinet until we're ready to go. "Finish the snacks so they're ready," he says to me.

"Does Pablo know where he's going?"

"Just to the doctor. That's all he knows. Most kids don't want to leave home even if they're being abused."

"Why does he keep running away then?"

"I think it's instinctual but maybe counterintuitive, being that he's so young."

"Dang. You are a psychologist's son. So where am I on your psychology scan? Healthy? Not so much?"

"It's a curse hearing so much about the human brain and all that can go wrong with it. You never look at people the same. Get the snacks over to the classroom and let's get out of here before Libby realizes we're missing."

I pause at the table because my heart is pounding. "I could lose everything over this. My parents would be livid." My stomach is churning at the thought, yet still I know I'm going to do it, if only because there might be no one else for the boy. Clearly Libby doesn't see what's happening at his house as a problem. And maybe it's not, but . . .

"I told you to stay here. I can handle it," J.C. says. "I have the perfect excuse. I'm going to get my permanent cast on. Just tell everyone here that the swelling went down and you're out of it altogether."

"They don't put them on that quickly." I pause, realizing I have no idea what I'm talking about. I'm only stalling for an answer from above. "Do they?" As I see the determined look on J.C.'s face, I know I can't let him go without me. He is one big Band-Aid, and his brain is muddled from the pain meds. I can't exactly let him drive in that condition, and I can't let Pablo go back to that angry man without checking things first. I'm what you'd call "between a rock and a hard place."

J.C. opens the cabinet, sweeps up Pablo in his arm, and comes toward me. He kisses me on the cheek. "I'll be back. Just cover for me."

My stomach is in knots. I look outside the door. Libby is nowhere in sight and neither is Pablo's stepfather. "I can't let you drive. Just wait in the house while I deliver the snacks and ask Claire to cover for me just in case we're not back by lunch."

"What are you two up to?"

"Ahh!" I squeal, nearly jumping out of my skin at the sight of Claire. "What are you doing sneaking up on us?"

"I thought you two might be necking," Claire jokes. She's dressed like beautiful Queen Esther and has black kohl eyeliner and bloodred lips—and it's a look that works for her. She's got such innocent eyes, you'd never guess the trouble she's capable of. I don't know why she's my friend, quite frankly. I'd look like the bride of Frankenstein dressed like that.

"Claire, you have to do me a favor. Can you serve the

snacks and lunch? The potatoes are in the oven and need to be turned off in half an hour."

"Where are you going?"

"I'd rather not tell you. The less you know, the better."

"Oh, this sounds good. Do tell."

"Claire! Will you do the snacks or not?"

"Done. It's done. I know nut-ting." She crunches a celery stick.

"Don't eat any more of those. They're counted out."

"All right. Who's the kid?"

I stare guiltily at Pablo. "You never saw him."

"What kid?" she asks. "I never saw a kid."

"Let's go." I push J.C. toward the door. He checks to make sure the coast is clear and limps quickly to his rental car. He unlocks the compact yellow box car and I take my place behind the wheel. "I don't have an international driver's license."

"You don't need one as long as you have yours from home. Besides, we're kidnapping a child from his guardian. A driver's license is the last thing you should be worried about."

At that, I fire up the engine and slowly back out of the dirt drive until we're on the dirt road. "Which way?"

"Right. We're going straight into town. Just follow the road."

"Doesn't he need a car seat?"

"Daisy, just drive."

"Maybe they don't do anything about child abuse in this country. Won't his stepfather say he just deserved it for running off? That he was trying to teach him a lesson?" I speak out every fear I have, and the roll of J.C.'s eyes is enough to tell me he doesn't need my kind of assistance.

"I want to know that nothing's broken on this kid, Daisy, and if you're afraid, turn around and I'll go myself."

"I'm not afraid. I am afraid," I keep repeating.

"I have a sixth sense about these things, Daisy. I can't explain it, but this kid needs our help, and I wouldn't feel right if I left the country without checking on his welfare."

"I know it." I stare into J.C.'s beautiful eyes. There's a warmth there that seems to ooze from every perfect pore. But I always put too much faith in cute guys. Never enough in myself. It's a character flaw, I think. God's the only one worthy of true devotion. "I wouldn't be here if I didn't believe your sixth sense. There's a reason that child keeps running from home, and his stepfather not letting him come to Vacation Bible School doesn't speak highly of the man."

He smiles tenderly and Pablo looks at me. "*Bonita*."

"Thank you, Pablo. *Muy guapo*." I rub his chin.

"Ah, you understand enough Spanish when it suits you," J.C. says. "Some charmer tells you that you're beautiful and you understand that."

"*Sí*, you're very handsome too." I rub J.C.'s chin in the same fashion. "Is someone feeling left out?"

"*Mi chica*," J.C. says to Pablo. "*Mi chica*."

Pablo laughs and pats his chest. "*Mi chica*."

"Turn here!" J.C. says at the last minute, and I squeal a turn into the medical clinic's parking lot. He starts to laugh. "You're a terrible driver."

"Yeah, well, you're a terrible navigator. Heard of a warning?"

He continues to laugh, which lights up his whole face. "Come on, we don't have much time if you're going to get back. Hopefully they'll have a nurse who can sit with him so we don't get caught." J.C. lifts himself out of the passenger seat and then grabs Pablo in his good arm.

"Do you want me to take him? I have a hip I can rest him on at least."

"Good point."

"*Quantos años?*" I ask Pablo as I lift him.

Pablo holds up four fingers. He doesn't even look two, and I start to worry that J.C.'s premonition is more than correct, it's spot-on. This boy doesn't look older than a fresh-walking toddler, and yet he's still in a diaper (today he has on a dirty polo shirt as well as my Pepperdine sweatshirt).

J.C. gives me a knowing glance and we hustle into the clinic, which is little more than a packed room with hard chairs and a series of white doors, one with a banker's window. I sit down with Pablo, and J.C. grabs a form and a clipboard. He whispers to the woman in white behind the counter, and I catch her glance at Pablo and nod her head. The only word I hear J.C. say is "hurry," and the only word I hear from her is "*policía*."

I tighten my arms around the little boy and start to sing quietly in his ear. He snuggles closer to me, and it grips my heart each time he does it. The way he cuddles up to a perfect stranger like he's so starved for affection—it makes my heart squeeze with emotion. Part of me wants to grab him up and run like the wind with him and give him all the love he deserves, but then I remember I don't know anything, really. We only have our suspicions, which could be completely off, and pretending to be the heroes, we could actually be the villains in this little guy's life. The police might not believe our story, and with the translation problems and differing laws, who knows what could happen to us?

Looking at J.C., so sure in the way he fills out the form and spoke to the triage gal, gives me absolute confidence in him, and I hope it's well founded. I have been known to trust the wrong sorts of people—especially when they're boy-band good-looking, so I hope I don't finish my travel journey in the pokey for international kidnapping.

J.C. sits next to us and takes Pablo from my arms. Pablo is nearly asleep. "It's going to be awhile. There's a long procedure, and the police will have to be called."

"The police? They're going to call Libby. Or worse, my parents." I start to imagine the scenario. My years in an Argentine prison with scary women who threaten to cut me.

He shakes his head. "No, they're not going to call Libby. Listen to me, you're going to take the car back to the mission. Tell Libby that my arm was killing me and you had to run me back to the clinic because I was going to drive myself, I was so in agony. Tell her the medications weren't working at all, and I needed something. I'll take care of this, and I'll either find a ride back or I'll call the mission when I'm done here. Classes should be finished by then, so you can come and get me after dinner."

"After dinner? That's hours from now. I haven't even served lunch! What if you need someone to back up your story? You don't want them to think you kidnapped him."

"If I kidnapped him, I wouldn't have brought him to a clinic, where the police would be called, would I? Go back and fix lunch so that Libby is none the wiser. That's the most sensible thing you can do for all of us."

"Maybe your Spanish isn't as good as you think it is. Maybe you told them something that gave rise to suspicion."

J.C. grins and grabs my knee, making me giggle instantly. "I'm sorry, I'm ticklish."

He squeezes my knee again, which gives rise to uncontrollable laughter. "Stop it." I look at all the faces staring at me. "People are watching. Stop it."

He does it again, and Pablo pops up from his near-sleep and laughs.

"Now look what you did!"

"It was worth it. From the first moment I met you, the only time I've ever seen you let down your guard and not worry is when you wolfed down half my sandwich. Since then you've been a bundle of nerves. Quit worrying! God says we can't add an hour to our life by worrying."

"I know, but it's what I do best. I'm good at worrying."

He shakes his head. "No, what you do best is giggle. Well, you make a mean peanut butter celery stalk too."

"What about you? Your arm has to be hurting from being in that position for so long, and that's not even mentioning your swollen foot."

"*No bonita*—pretty—when you nag," he says.

"I want to stay," I tell him truthfully.

"Only because you're not thinking about Libby's reaction at this very moment."

"No. I'm thinking I want to be here to support you."

"Libby will call your parents," he says.

I bound out of my chair. "Point taken. I'm going."

J.C. moves out from under Pablo and stands alongside me. He looks like he had to be very popular in high school, which immediately makes me want to forget every tingly feeling I'm having. If we were not thrust together under the eyes of Libby the scary missionary, he wouldn't have given me a second's notice.

"I might never get another chance to do this, and I promised myself I was not going to let shyness stop me on this trip. I am going to be the new and improved J.C. Wiggs."

"Do what?" He's so close to me that I can feel his soft breath against my lips. The room is filled with people, but it's as if we're time traveling and there's no one in the space but J.C. and me.

"I wanted to kiss you from the moment you stole my sandwich." He presses his lips against mine and stares at me. I can't think of anything to say, and he does it again. There are a few whistles and catcalls around us, but this doesn't thwart him either. He kisses me a third time. "Go back and cover for me," he whispers. He nods in satisfaction. "It was a good kiss."

I nod, unable to say anything.

"I should have asked to kiss you," he says in front of everyone, and I hope to high heaven no one understands English. "Is it all right that I kissed you?"

I feel myself nod again like an overanimated bobble head, but I don't even have the presence of mind to worry. I'm too busy floating.

11

My Life: Stop—July 8

Factoid: A kiss is just a kiss. Except it's not when it's in a foreign country and with someone I actually want to kiss me. It takes on a romantic hue. Even in a sterile doctor's environment.

I sit here on Claire's cot in utter amazement. I can't believe we got away with our deceitful yet honorable plan. I never get away with anything! Not even when I'm innocent in the matter have I ever gotten away with something. I'm almost afraid I'm going to lead a life of crime after this because I feel giddy that I didn't get caught and astonished that Libby knows nothing about it whatsoever. I came home expecting to find her waiting for me, tapping her toe, but nothing. The room was silent, the snacks were gone, and lunch was about to be served.

Now, if you add in the fact that J.C. kissed me on this stealth mission, it's almost like I'm invisible. In a good way, though. Like a superhero way. A kiss—the one thing that Libby warned us would get us thrown out of the mission and we wouldn't get our scholarships and our lives would be virtually ruined. But that didn't happen. Nothing happened. I just told Libby the story about J.C. going back to the medical clinic, and she believed it and that was the end of it. I served lunch. I served dinner. I cleaned up dinner, and . . . nothing happened!

Pablo's stepfather did come searching for him again, and this time the man was really frantic. No doubt Pablo's mother was due home soon and he'd have some explaining to do. Libby was worried too and offered to call the police for him, but Pablo's stepfather turned her down. She sent the guys out looking for the boy, and it really took all my willpower not to spill everything. Knowing the guys were out looking for someone they'd never find filled me with guilt, but the truth is, I worried about J.C. more, so I kept my mouth clamped shut.

My throat was so constricted the whole time, I worried I'd been bitten by some rare and venomous snake without knowing it and the venom had taken over my vocal cords. Knowing J.C. might be in danger, I stayed quiet and let the guys go out looking rather than save them the trouble.

I focused my thoughts on Pablo's bruised thigh and his

small size for his age. I tried to calculate in my head if the man had it in him to beat a child, but who knows what a monster looks like? They look like you and me, right? So how would I know? I decided it was better to leave it to the police. In a way, I hoped his stepfather was innocent. I mean, he looked exactly like I'd imagine a child abuser would look, and that seemed so very obvious.

"What are you writing?" Claire climbs up the ladder just as I slam my journal shut. "About the hot kisses you and J.C. shared while we were all in the classroom?"

I shrug. "What? No. Just what's happening here at the mission."

"So does that mean there were hot kisses?" Claire giggles at her joke.

"We couldn't keep our hands off each other," I tell her, and we both giggle.

"Seriously, what is happening? What are you writing in there?" She sits on the cot and curls her legs up underneath her. "Is there romance? Maybe a small spark of romance?"

"Not unless I want to lose my scholarship, there isn't."

It's not lying exactly. It's omitting the truth so that I don't hold Claire liable for knowing a thing. That way she's in no danger with Libby and I'm in no danger for her being unable to keep her mouth shut.

The phone rings and I startle at the unfamiliar sound.

"What is up with you? You're as jumpy as a frog in Angels Camp."

"Shh!" I hiss, trying to overhear Libby on the phone. She's making sounds of agreement as if she's listening to a litany of details. I find myself praying for J.C. and hoping that Pablo is safe and hasn't been sent home if the house is unsafe. In a way, I hope J.C. was wrong and it's all a giant misunderstanding, and that Pablo is home safe and cuddled into a warm bed.

"*Sí. Gracias. Muchas gracias.*" Libby hangs up the phone. "Daisy!" she shouts.

"Yes," I purr as innocently as possible.

"Go pick up J.C. He's done at the clinic." I look down over the wooden rail. There's nothing on her face that gives any sign she knows a thing other than I'm to go pick up J.C.

"I'll go," Hank says, slamming a book shut. "I don't want her out by herself at night."

"She volunteered herself to be in this situation, she can go. You're tired from the day's work. She'll be fine."

Hank meekly opens his book again, and I scramble to get my shoes on.

"Do you want me to go with you?" Claire asks.

"No," I say too quickly, because the ride back is all J.C. and I will have to get our story straight. "J.C. will be embarrassed to have you see him hurting. He's used to me seeing him all groggy from the meds this morning. You just stay here and get ready for the morning. I imagine Queen Esther's part will be even bigger tomorrow. Wouldn't want you to forget your lines."

She holds up a script. "Totally. It's really challenging my inner actor to speak in another language. It's like doing Shakespeare."

"Except Shakespeare's in English."

"Yeah, but ye olde English. Hardly the same thing."

"Right," I say, sliding into my sweater.

Claire stands beside me and whispers in my ear, "You may be able to fool Libby, but I know you're up to something. You're a terrible liar."

I swallow the huge lump in my throat. "The less you know, the better. Believe that."

"I'm certain that's true, which is why I'm not asking you."

I grin at her and grab her wrist. "See ya soon."

I clamber down the ladder and meet Libby's suspicious glare. "If I find out you know anything about Pablo, you're done here."

"Who?"

Libby purses her lips. "There's just something I don't trust about you, Daisy Crispin. You have that same glint in your eye that your father always had, and I never trusted him either."

"Then there's nothing I can do that will disappoint you or, in effect, please you, right? I can't win here, and what's different about me this time is that I'm not even going to try. Not because I don't respect you, but because I'm a good worker and I'll do my best regardless. You're very good at what you do, Libby. Someday maybe you'll realize others do it just as well, but differently."

"I doubt that."

So did I, but it felt satisfying saying what I thought anyway. Libby didn't seem like the sort to ever change her thinking, no matter how much evidence there was to the contrary. Some people were married to their ignorance and I chalk Libby up to that category. I wonder if people ever think, *I hope heaven is big enough for the two of us*. Because Libby makes me think that way. I hope she's on the upper east side and I'm on the lower west side, or however it works. I hope she's in another wing. Which I know cannot be garnering me any more jewels in my crown, but neither can lying about my feelings.

I grab the keys and rush to the vehicle as if I'm an escaped convict, and in many ways I suppose I am. I turn on the radio, because let's face it, there's nothing cheerier than a little Latino music when you're frantic and fearing a foreign penal system, is there? I'm thinking not.

When I get to the medical clinic, I drive up to the darkened building and there's not a soul in sight. Truthfully, it looks like a scene out of a horror movie—not that my mom's ever let me see one, but I've seen the commercials. I start to get out of the car, then think better of it. J.C. is nowhere in sight. I press all the locks down on the car doors and pray for some sort of divine guidance. "God, what do I do now?"

There's silence. Silence and crickets.

"I don't know what to do," I say aloud. "God, J.C. didn't tell me what to do if this didn't work out, and if I come back without him, Libby will know for certain we were up to something."

More crickets. It slowly dawns on me that I can actually smell myself sitting in this car. The most gorgeous guy I've ever met kissed me today, and I smell like a dirty puppy because water is so scarce here. Like fire and compassion are. I'm disgusting. Maybe J.C.'s nose didn't work right after he got hit, or maybe we both smelled so ripe that we didn't notice the stench of the other. Maybe it's like caveman love or something virtually unknown to those of us from America.

There's a rap on my window, and I scream as my imagination runs wild. I look up and see a policeman showing me his badge. Lord forgive me, but I've seen too many bad *Lifetime* movies and I don't want to roll down the window. He knocks again.

"Daisy," he says. "Daisy Crispin?" He rolls the *r* in my name, and it's like Antonio Banderas in my mind's eye.

I roll the window down a crack.

"*Tu amigo?* J.C.?"

"*Sí? Mi español es muy mal*," I tell him, as if I need to. He can hear I'm not really speaking his language, can he not?

He motions for me to follow him in his cruiser. I toss up another set of desperate prayers and wait for him to start up his car. He slowly rolls onto the road and I follow at a safe pace behind him. I have the most irritating thought: would I have trusted J.C. so easily if he didn't look like he did? What if this is all part of a deep, international kidnapping scheme where I am taken and sold into a . . . I shudder, not wanting to finish the thought. What if J.C. were a complete troll with a white man fro and a scruffy beard? Would I have said, "Oh yes, J.C., I'll help you kidnap this child because of a preconceived notion you have in your head after being raised by a mother who could star on *Intervention*"? Yes, another heaping helping of boy-crazy, inane decisions for me. Please. The police officer is in a police car, but aren't foreign cops on the take? Seriously, isn't that the crux of every major thriller?

A brightly lit building is up ahead, and I've never been so grateful to see civilization. There are small stores, still open, a petrol station, and a very modern building that appears to be a full-sized hospital. The policeman gets out of his vehicle and saunters over to my car. Why do all cops walk that way? Is it in the code book or something?

I step out of my car and he hands me a strip of paper with English writing on it. It's signed by J.C.

"Thank you." I wave the paper. "*Gracias.*"

I enter the building and ask for directions. "*Cuatro once?*"

The nurse, all dressed in white, points me to the elevators, which don't exactly look like they're up to American code, so I ask for the stairs. She points in the other direction, and I climb up four flights of stairs until I match the numbers on the outside of the rooms to the one on my strip of paper. I peek into the room and gasp in horror. J.C.'s one eye peers out from behind strips of bandages.

"What happened to your gorgeous face?" I run to the bedside.

"Hopefully it's still under the bandages." He smiles with a cut lip. "You think my face is gorgeous, Daisy?"

I touch his bruised face as gently as I can around the bandages, but he still flinches. "Don't pretend you've never looked into a mirror, J.C. You know what you look like. I shouldn't have to spell it out for you. Who did this to you?"

He grins. "Yes, spell it out for me. It rushes the healing."

"J.C." My body tightens at the sight of him, and I wish I could take some of his pain from him. I try to make light of the situation to improve his spirits. "You look like you should be answering to the name of Lucky about now. Have you always had this kind of luck, or is it just my entrance into your life?"

"Don't make me laugh. It hurts." He grabs his stomach with his good arm. "You should see the other guy."

"Does he look worse than you?"

"He doesn't even have a scratch, but in my defense, I

didn't see him coming. He came up all ninja on me from behind and I didn't get one good punch in. I hope you don't need me to defend your honor because I'm not all that good in a fight. In my head I was Superman until it came time to prove it."

"You're in luck. My honor is fine and not in need of defending. Regardless of what Libby thinks of me."

"Would you touch my face again? That was sweet, and I want to take something good home from Argentina that doesn't come in the form of cotton bandages."

I allow my fingers to gently graze his cheek and he winces. "The green of your eyes is even greener with the black eye. Very hot, but I'll take the regular green to have you not beaten to a pulp."

He laughs again. "Stop it!"

"Were you robbed?"

"Pablo's stepfather found me." He says it simply, as if he deserved the beating. "Something tells me Pablo's mother wasn't all too happy to find the little guy missing."

"But he's okay?"

"Pablo's fine."

I brush the backs of my fingers softly along his hand and marvel at how brave J.C. was through all this. He didn't know the law, but it didn't stop him from doing what was right. I honor him for that, and I wonder if he hadn't been here if I would have tried not to notice Pablo's bruise. If I would have run from the conflict because of Libby and her beliefs about me. In short, I wonder if J.C. wasn't sent here to show me what a hero looks like.

I've never been more myself and tried less with a guy, and it feels fantastic to actually be liked for who I am—but I have to keep in mind that it could be the head injury, am I right? He's changed my whole outlook on life in two days. I never want to struggle to be accepted again. Not with someone I consider a boyfriend.

Then I notice his expression. He's got that leaving look I've grown accustomed to.

"J.C., you didn't bring me all the way out here to tell me you're not coming back with me to the mission, right?"

He's silent, and I feel my eyes springing moisture. He takes my hand in his, which puts me at ease. "You'll be fine. I'll see you at school in a month and a half. You can find your own trouble without me. But I can't go back to the mission for obvious reasons. If Pablo's stepfather is around, Libby will get blamed for all of this. Plus how do I explain coming back from the clinic looking worse than when I went in?"

I grip his hand. "Please, J.C. You have to come back. You can just hide out in the house like you've been doing. I'd recognize Pablo's stepfather and I'd warn you."

"I wanted to say goodbye to you in person. That's why I asked you out here. Six weeks and we'll be together again."

"Libby doesn't like me, and you're the only thing that's made the work there bearable."

"It's five days, and if I thought you were in any danger, I wouldn't leave."

I grin at the idea but, against my better judgment, decide to complain more. "I'm not working with the kids. I'm in that kitchen all alone and I still have five days left. Can't you just convalesce in the kitchen like you've been doing? Maybe sneak me a peck on the cheek now and again?" I give him my best puppy dog eyes.

His eyebrows rise and fall. "That hurt. I do like the idea of you taking care of me, I'm not going to lie. But it's not safe for me to be seen at the mission. Pablo's stepfather doesn't know where I found Pablo or why I took him to the clinic, and that's best. In fact, he tried to accuse me of taking Pablo and hurting the boy myself. Luckily, Pablo had already shown them what happened and kept saying 'Papa,' so I was free and clear. He trusted the officer right away, and he'd already told the nurse his story when I was with him. His bruises were too old to be from someone who took him that day regardless. I probably wasn't even in the country when they happened."

"What's going to happen to Pablo?"

"He's safe. He's with the authorities, and they had a female police officer who was so nice to him. She brought him a stuffed animal, so he snuggled into her just like he did you and me. With all the Latino charm that kid has, he's going to have few troubles in life once he's away from this stepfather of his. I don't think Pablo's mom is actually married to the guy. She'll have to get rid of him or risk losing Pablo."

"I'm so happy to hear it."

"The reason I brought you out here is so that I could see your face before I left Argentina, and also I wanted to tell you what to say to Libby so that she doesn't know about any of this. Plus I told you I was going to call, and I wasn't about to ditch you after that tool didn't show up with the candy."

J.C. still has hold of my hand, and right now I can't imagine leaving him here in a foreign hospital by himself. "I was angry that he didn't show up with the candy because it was a pattern. I do what I say I'm going to do, so maybe I expect too much of others."

"I do what I say I'm going to do. Except I can't come back like I promised, so I wanted you to know why. There's no telling what that guy is capable of. He pummeled me when I left the clinic. Actually waited for me and had some idea I was there. The cops were right behind me and they arrested him, but not before the guy got his meaty fists on me from behind."

"The cops had too many doughnuts?"

"I know, right? My grandmother is getting my flight home rescheduled, but I need to get back to town tomorrow. I can't run the risk of going back to the mission because if Pablo's stepfather sees me there, the mission could take the brunt of his rage, and we all know that would not end well."

"For Libby or Pablo's stepfather?"

"Good point. If it's not too much to ask, I want you to call your friend, what's-his-name. The one who didn't show up. I want you to ask him to come and take me to Buenos Aires. He can pick up my stuff and the rental car and come get me."

My joy dies. "I just told you he's not reliable, but if he does come, it will be in his own car. Maybe one of the other guys can take the rental back to the airport when they go."

"That works for me. Besides, this guy won't let you down twice. Not when you tell him what happened. His country's honor is at stake. He has to know you don't dis a beautiful girl twice."

I bypass his compliment in favor of worrying about Max's reliability. "What if you miss your flight? Max is always late." Naturally, I don't mention the fact that it's totally weird to have two guys I've kissed by choice (Chase, my kindergarten crush, kissed me in some kind of funky mercy move in the school quad) in the same vehicle and capable of comparing notes.

"Yeah, Max. He can go by the mission, pick up my stuff, and not raise any suspicions with Libby. If Libby sees me like this, she'll know we were lying to her."

"But my parents are in town. They could—"

"No parental units." J.C. shakes his head.

"J.C., you're being ridiculous. Did you get hit in the head?"

"I did, actually. A couple of times, but this isn't the end for us, right? We're going to see each other in Malibu in a month and a half. We'll each go to the business student mixer, maybe dance or share some punch . . ."

"That would be nice."

"I'm not meeting your parents looking like a thug on the bad end of a street fight. Plus I can't wear shoes because my foot looks diseased from a scorpion sting, so they might think I have some rare disease and assume it's something I could give to you. I think you'll agree that's not the best way to introduce myself to your parents, wouldn't you?"

"I can go back and get your stuff. I can drive you. I'll just turn in the rental car and get a shuttle or something back."

"Yeah, and Libby will be more than likely to sign your scholarship paperwork with all that time off, won't she?"

"What about Claire?"

"Your chaperone?" he asks. "I want Max."

"In a weird way, I think Libby wants me to get caught being up to something. Why would she send me out to pick you up all by myself if she didn't?"

"So you'll find Max? Here's my cell number. Give it to him and tell him I'll pay him whatever his time is worth."

"You don't think that's . . . I don't know, kind of weird?"

"Weird? Why? He's from here. You know him. You won't vouch for me that my story is true?"

"Of course I will, but Max dumped me. At least I think he dumped me, I'm not exactly sure. What makes you think he'd want to do me a favor?"

"Leave that to me. He didn't dump you. He isn't reliable, right?"

"Well, I thought we had a romance and apparently we didn't, and he could have had the courtesy to tell me on Skype, but he waited and just ditched me one night in Argentina. I think."

"So he's an idiot. He can still drive and he knows where the mission is. Two things in my favor. And if he thinks he's still your boyfriend, I'll set him straight on that account too. See? It's all good."

"I don't know how to reach him," I point out. "He never gave me his cell phone number."

"Claire can email him on her smartphone. I'll bet she has a way to find him."

"You have an answer for everything."

"I know, isn't it great?" J.C. grins. "I've been waiting around all day. I had nothing to do but think, and this is the plan I came up with. A taxi would have to take me back to the mission. If one of you leaves the mission, it will only raise Libby's suspicions, and like I said, she's better off ignorant all the way around."

"I was sort of hoping the stepfather was innocent."

"Me too. Wait a minute, why?"

"Because he looked like a child abuser. I was thinking that made it too easy, the fact that he looked like what I pictured a child abuser to be."

"I don't know if they have a version of our cop shows down here, but I guess TV gets it right sometimes. Though I know from my mother's practice, abusers come in all packages."

"What if I can't find Max?"

"Then I guess you'll have to do it. At least bring my stuff here. Then I could catch a car to Buenos Aires, but I really don't want to take the chance, Daisy. If something happened to you, I'd never forgive myself."

I nod.

"You'd better get back. Libby will be looking for you."

Instinctively my body pulls closer to J.C.'s. It doesn't want to move. For the first time in my life, I think romance doesn't have to be so hard. Sometimes it blossoms out of a natural friendship and an inexplicable bond.

"You have to go, Daisy."

I stare into his one good eye and still can't explain how I got here. How I feel such a loss after two days. He leans in toward me and gently presses his lips to mine. I kiss him back gently so as not to split his lip again and stand awkwardly. "How will I know you're okay?"

"I'll find a way to let you know. Do you have a pen?"

I dig through the drawer beside him and find a golf pencil, then write down his information. His cell phone, his home phone, his address, his Facebook name, his Skype account. Basically, any way he can possibly be tracked down, I now have it.

"There's a reason all this happened."

I nod, unable to talk for fear I'll blubber.

"Call me the minute you get stateside."

I press my lips to his one last time and suddenly feel nothing has ever been wrong in the world and never will be again.

This is what it feels like to be loved back. I hope, because it's fantastic and sans drama.

My Life: Stop—July 8 and 9

Random factoid: Nice guys don't always finish last.

I was numb to the fear of entering Libby's lair. I felt no pain as I relived J.C.'s gentle kiss and heard his soft words again in my memory. But it was none of those things that made me believe J.C. is special. It was his actions, pure and simple. He stepped up to the plate when he had every reason not to. He overlooked the humiliation of calling Max because it was better for everyone if Max found his way back to the mission and kept Libby in the dark as to the dangers lurking just outside the compound.

I was dancing a waltz from a 1950s musical by the time I got to the mission's door. Holding on to J.C.'s secret has made me feel special and important, as if I'm a special agent on assignment. Anything I can do to steer clear of my reality is a bonus at this point. So important, in fact, that I didn't even want to tell Claire what I was up to, but that proved impossible since I had to reach Max, and she had the international cell phone that made emailing him possible. Because Claire has everything that makes life easier. I'd say, on average, her life has to be a good 99.8 percent easier than mine.

I emailed Max, and within an hour he emailed me back. (Go figure. Maybe he's feeling guilty.) He's picking up J.C.'s stuff and then J.C. Why now? Why does Max come through for me when it's the most awkward situation for me?

Guys. I will never understand them!

Libby's calling, gotta run.

So now it's morning. It doesn't seem like J.C.'s presence is missed by anyone but me, and since Libby is not all that interested in me, she never asked about J.C. But considering he was my only company in the cold cave, I miss him more than I could have imagined. And not in a romantic, pathetic way either. Just in an "I'm lonely and no one here likes me" way.

Claire and Libby seem to be besties for reasons I can't fathom. I actually hear Libby giggling at Claire's jokes and it's like a slap in the face. I know that's totally immature, like Claire can't be friends with her and friends with me, but hello! The woman has totally threatened my college education unless I meet her exacting standards.

Incidentally, I do realize that it's stupid to call my journal a travel journal. I could be anywhere. Coming through the beautiful but crowded center of Buenos Aires and passing the water and palm trees was the extent of the travel portion of my first international trip.

My fortunes do not change. Trouble follows me, and if I've learned anything about traveling, it's that I bring my luck with me. Which is a good lesson, I figure. It's going to save me a lot of money in the future, as I won't be traveling. I can just stay at home. I know it's not scriptural to believe in luck, and technically I don't, but I sure seem to have this thing I don't believe in and a lot of it.

I just heard a car! Max must be here! My heart is pounding at the thought, and I'm not sure if it's because I'm anxious to see Max or I'm anxious that he's going to see J.C., or all of the above. But I don't have time to think about it now.

Climbing down the ladder's rungs, I gather up J.C.'s bags near the sofa and head toward the door. It's open a crack when I reach it, and Max is standing outside in jeans and a plaid cotton shirt, his fist poised to knock.

"Hi," I say to him with just a bit of a chill in my voice, but his deep, espresso eyes melt me every time. I wish I wasn't so shallow, but looking at their depth, I want to know everything stirring behind them. Though he's probably thinking nothing more than, *What is wrong with that girl?*

"Hi," he says briskly—just a few degrees colder than the greeting I gave him. "I'm here for that guy's stuff."

"Yeah. It's right here." I hand him the backpack and bedroll. "Max . . ." I linger on his name, willing him to look at me. He finally does. "I really appreciate this. You have no idea how much this is helping me."

"Whatever." His terse answer ticks me off.

"Are you mad at me? Because you're sort of the one who failed to show up and do what you promised. Not that I'm not grateful you're here now and all, but you did promise me dinner and then with no explanation—" *Oh my goodness, I sound like a nagging wife!*

He shakes his head. "I'm not mad at you, and you know if I could have been here, I would have been. I'm mad at me."

"You are?"

"You like this J.C.?"

"It's not about that, Max. We need your help. Both of us. I don't have time to explain now, but I will." I keep looking over his shoulder, hoping that Libby won't come out and accuse me of setting up a dating service—or worse—in her kitchen. "Is your mother all right? I thought of her immediately when you didn't show."

He hikes the backpack over his shoulder. "She's fine. She has bad days and good. Right now she's good."

"I'm so glad!" But he still doesn't tell me what's wrong with her. I suppose it's none of my business anyway.

"I guess we'll have to trust each other then. You have your reasons, I have mine." He tucks the bedroll under his arm. "I have to go."

"That's it?" I ask him, while at the same time checking the schoolroom frantically for any sign of class being over. I follow him to his car.

He lifts the trunk and shoves J.C.'s stuff into the small compartment. He slams the trunk, and I let my breath out, thankful that he's around the corner and out of sight from the classroom and Libby's prying eyes. I pad after him and try to decipher what he really thinks of my asking him this favor.

"Thanks for doing this, Max."

He looks around me. "I'd better get out of here before your boss sees me. I assume you don't want me seen."

"Yeah." I look away when I answer, ashamed that I'm asking for a favor and wanting to hide him at the same time.

Max looks at me with those intense, roasted-espresso eyes that seem to force truth out of me—not that I'm a liar. "It seems you feel strongly about getting this guy out of town."

"I do."

Max scratches the nape of his neck and seems to want to say something, but keeps stopping himself.

"Just say it," I tell him.

"Say what?"

"Whatever it is you need to say to me."

He grabs the back of his neck. "I'd rather not."

"I wish you'd just say it. Something stopped you from doing what you said you would, and I think it would be better to just spit it out than string me along while I'm down here." As much as I don't want to hear there's someone else or that he's just not into me, there's also a deep need to understand.

"I'd better get your friend before he misses his plane."

"Were we ever . . . you know . . . did I imagine we had a relationship when there wasn't one?" I exhale audibly. "There, I said it."

"If we did, you seem to have gotten over it quickly enough. Already asking me to chauffeur your new boyfriend around. It's like you didn't even wait until the body was cold."

My mouth is open and there are sputtering sounds coming out, but I can't quite come up with words. What I want to say is some movie quote I always hear from my dad: "What we have here is a failure to communicate."

"Me? You're the one who ditched me without so much as a phone call, and now I know you could have reached Claire at any time."

"Claire. Not you. You didn't have a phone."

"But you brought her here. You knew she was with me."

He ponders this for a minute, and I fill in the silence.

"You've done everything you can to avoid me since the last day of school, from not having time to Skype to not answering emails. And when I came down here you were all warm and cozy until you ditched me without so much as a phone call. I just don't get it. If you dumped me, I wish you'd had the guts to tell me so outright."

"I told you, I had something to do. You're the one who got cozy with a guy you barely know, nursing him and taking care of his ride to the airport."

I step closer to him. "I'm sure you did have something to do, but you know what? It made me realize something."

"What's that?"

"If I have a boyfriend, I think I should know it, not just guess all the time where I stand. I think that wouldn't make for a very happy life."

"All you had to do was ask!" Max shouts.

"I shouldn't have to ask. Isn't that the equivalent of begging?" What is it with passive guys who make girls do all the work? There has to be a guy out there who thinks I'm worth chasing. Asking for affection is beyond pathetic, and my daddy didn't raise me to beg for a hero. If he's a hero, he'll chase me.

"J.C. doesn't make you beg, is that it? You know this guy, what, two days, and you know everything about him and think he's never going to let you down? Maybe he doesn't have a mother with hepatitis to take care of, did you ever think of that? That would lighten a guy's load."

"You're not going to make me feel guilty for asking. You're jealous. That's all this is about. Your ego is bruised." I want to ask him how it feels, but that would feel far too good and then I'd have guilt.

"Daisy!"

I hear my name shouted, and my stomach clenches. "Go!

It's Libby," I say to Max. "I'm right here," I call out and rush around the corner only to run smack-dab into Libby.

"Come here, young man," she yells at Max, and I see him pause and look behind him at the car, as if he's thinking whether he should make a run for it. He decides against it, and I hear my heart pounding in my ears.

"Yes?" Max leans on the roof of his car with one elbow on the door.

"What are you doing here? Did you come to pick up Daisy? Daisy, are you planning on leaving us without notice?"

"No! Of course not."

"What? No. She's working for the week," Max concurs.

"I can't use her here. I've already warned her about my rules, and it seems like she's determined to play by a different set. Take her with you." She waves her hand toward me as though I'm yesterday's rubbish.

"No," Max tells Libby in a pleading voice. "I came . . . I came to bring her sweets for the kids, but then I realized I left them in my van. I brought the wrong car." He slaps his forehead, and it's clear Libby doesn't believe a word of his story. I suppose I can take solace in the fact that Max is a terrible liar. Maybe that's why he's said so little to me all along.

"Daisy, why don't you go and grab your stuff. I think I'll handle the cooking from here."

"But I—"

"You'd better get back to America if you plan to finish your scholarship experience. I've already had one of you go AWOL on me, so it's not a surprise you'd both go. Don't get me wrong, I'm grateful you brought me the best Queen Esther I've ever seen. I can't find fault in your best friend." She sings this as if she hasn't just kicked me out of her home and forgotten the reason I was able to come to Buenos Aires in the first place. I'm too stunned to feel anything but desperation for her to change her mind.

"Libby, you can't send me away. I have nowhere to go! My parents are in Buenos Aires and—"

"Someday you're going to look back on this and see that it was all for the best. Don't you remember how Saint Paul kicked Saint Mark off of the missionary tour and they doubled their coverage? God will use this. I'm certain of that much."

"Libby, why? I've done everything you asked of me and you know my mother!"

"I can't let that take my focus off the vision for the mission. We have enough help now, and I do think you'll agree you and I don't see eye to eye. I like things done a certain way and you don't seem to honor that. Let's part ways as friends, shall we? Friends who will meet again someday, God willing, in heaven." She holds out her hand to me.

"I'll get my stuff." I look at Max. "Will you wait?"

His cheek flinches, but I'm without options. Uncomfortable or not, Max is my ticket back to the safety of my parents, which reminds me of my failure but makes me glad I have a place to run.

"You expect Claire to stay then?" I ask Libby.

"She has her whole life to vacation. Right now she's doing God's work. The work he created her to do. She's a natural." Libby pulls her straggling blonde hair back into a ponytail, and I marvel at how easily she takes control of people around her.

I shouldn't feel betrayed by Claire, since Libby is answering for her, but I'm ashamed that I do. "I should talk with

Claire before I leave, though. She might need a ride, or not expect to be here alone."

At this, Max shakes his head impatiently and Libby crosses her arms. I run into the small house to grab my things and see Claire's upscale bags sitting beside them. I have to give her the choice, I think, as I gather up my stuff under one arm and climb down the ladder.

As I exit the door, I look to my right. Libby and Max are both staring at me, but I can't leave Claire without at least telling her I'm leaving. There's no reason for her to be here, and regardless of how Libby feels, Claire needs to make the choice.

I run across the field until I come to the classroom. Claire is in front of the children, dressed as Queen Esther with black kohl around her eyes and blood-red lipstick, in a costume that looks more Egyptian than biblical. She is speaking her lines in Spanish, and I can see she has the entire classroom mesmerized.

I tap the doorjamb and try to wait patiently until her scene is finished, but it's going on forever. "Pssst!" I try to grab her attention. "Pssst!"

Claire continues her lines as if she's on the London stage, and if she hears me, she makes no sign of it. Her theory that the show must go on is making me tense. But I wait until her line is finished and call out, "Claire!"

She hikes up her long gown and sways toward me. "What is it?" she hisses.

"Claire, Libby wants me to leave, and Max is outside waiting to take me back to Buenos Aires. Will you come?"

"Right now?" She glances back at the children.

"Max has to be back to town for something. Libby's made it clear that the time is now."

Claire brushes back her black bob to reveal sparkling, fake-gold earrings. "Daisy . . . there are four more days to go. I've learned all the lines."

"I don't have a choice, but you do. I'll support you either way."

"I can't leave yet. I promised Libby and the kids—" Claire motions toward the students. "What will they say if Esther doesn't finish the story?"

"You don't mind then?"

"I want to stay. I'm good at this, Daisy, and I love it. I'm happy here." She's near tears, as if I'm going to take something away from her.

"You can stay. I don't mind. I just wanted you to know I'm leaving and to make sure you didn't feel abandoned. You'll be the only girl left on the overnight staff."

"Libby's here."

That didn't matter when I was the only girl, but I suppose for the perfect Queen Esther, Libby will make an exception. "Yeah. I'll be at your hotel with my parents. You're sure you'll be okay without me here?"

"It doesn't sound like I have a choice," Claire says.

True. "Not if you want to finish."

"She's welcome." Libby interrupts me. "She hasn't given me a moment's trouble, and she's the best actress we've ever had in a role for the kids. They love her, and I'd be crushed if she left now."

The kids start to tug on Claire's robe as though she's Jesus himself. She smiles and bends down until she's surrounded by little figures glomming onto her. "I couldn't leave now."

"Then I have to run. There's something I have to do."

Libby's eyes narrow at my words, but I figure nothing I

say would surprise her now. She probably thinks Max and I are off on a romantic tryst. But it doesn't matter what she thinks. J.C.'s secret is keeping Libby safe, even if she doesn't know the truth. God knows the truth.

Claire nods. "I'll call you when the work week here is done." She bends down to the kids' level. "It's important to finish what I started."

"Yeah." I try to comprehend how Claire found the experience here to be so fulfilling while it was like serious dental work for me the entire time. "Call when you're ready."

Libby smirks at me, as if she's won over my best friend like we're in a bad junior high girl fight. I pray to find the right words and inner peace. "Thank you for your hospitality, Libby. I hope you have a wonderful and fruitful week here."

"Just remember, spiritual pride is a terrible character flaw to battle in this lifetime. I'll pray for you, Daisy."

"You do that," I say with all the sarcasm I can muster. I rush across the field to Max and get into the already running car. He doesn't even look at me, he just starts backing out.

As we're leaving, my parents pass us, pulling into the dirt lot in a rented yellow vehicle. "It's my parents! Max, stop the car."

He looks genuinely ticked off, but he stops the car. "Why don't you take your stuff and go with them?"

My mouth dangles open. "Max, you know why. Are you bailing on me?"

He sighs his annoyance. "Just hurry up. That guy is going to miss his flight."

I run to the passenger window and pant my desperation. I know what they must be thinking about me taking off with

Max in the middle of my work week. "Mom, Dad." I motion for them to roll down the window.

"Daisy, I have the best news!" my mother shouts.

"Mom, not now. Please listen. You have to trust me, but I have to go and I can't explain why right now. Libby kicked me out of the program, and I've got to get back to America and work full-time for the food bank to cover my ministry requirements. But there's something else I have to do before I go back to the hotel. Max is going to take me on an errand, and I need you to trust that he's the man for the job. And that I'll be safe with him."

"What do you mean she kicked you out?" My father shuts off the engine and steps out of the vehicle. He's staring at me over the roof of the car. He looks like he's ready to have Libby for lunch, and he starts to march across the field.

"Dad," I call after him. "Don't. You'll only make things worse, and Claire's staying. *Please.* Just trust me, I'll explain everything later. I promise, Max and I won't be alone for long, and this has nothing to do with us. We're not even a couple. Please believe me."

"What you're doing isn't dangerous, is it?"

"No. Not anymore. I just need to go."

Mom grabs my arm, and I notice she's wearing a silver ring decorated with her first initial. "Where did you get that?"

"Your father bought it for me in town. Isn't it beautiful?"

It's not, really, but my mom and I have never agreed on the definition of beauty. "Nice job, Dad. Tell me all about it at dinner, all right?"

"What time will you be back at the hotel? We'll head there now," my dad says.

I look at Max and then back to my parents. "I'll be there by six at the latest."

"Take our phone so we can reach you and we don't have to worry. You can call the hotel and leave us a message if you're delayed for any reason."

I nod and take the proffered cell phone. "Thanks Mom, Dad. Thanks for trusting me." I clutch the phone in my hand and walk toward Max. If I wanted closure, I sure did a good job of opening up yet another can of worms with J.C. And would Max remotely care about me if J.C. weren't in the picture?

I stare at him, trying to decipher his thoughts as I get into the car. His deep, dark eyes reveal nothing.

12

My skin feels like it's crawling with scorpions as Max and I hurtle toward town on the scarcely paved road. I figure I have precious few seconds to work this out with Max before J.C. comes into the picture. It's not exactly the prime place to have a DTR (define the relationship) conversation, especially when I think that definition is about who broke up with whom.

"Max, just so I know, if you dumped me, can you tell me why? I have this insane need to learn from my mistakes. Or yours, as the case may be, but I want to learn anyway."

"I don't know that we were really . . . you know, dating, to say *dumped*. That's a strong word."

"As in being left waiting for a gentleman caller who never came."

"Touché."

I'm feeling more desperate for answers as he speeds toward the hospital. "Can you slow down, Max? I'm trying to talk to you."

"I can't be late for your boyfriend. He's going to miss his plane."

I slump in my seat. I give up. Max is impossible, and

maybe, just maybe, it's totally him and not me at all. Without closure, that's the way I choose to see it. The dude has issues.

"If J.C. is my boyfriend, I made pretty fast work of him. I closed that deal quickly."

"Sarcasm noted," Max says. "I assumed I'd see you when you were back in town. You know I have a job, right?"

I would have assumed that too if you'd said it, rather than "I'll be out to see you." But I don't say this. It sounds too volatile, too angry, as if his visit meant far too much to me. Let him wallow in the fact that J.C. was present. I don't want to chase a guy like Max makes me chase him. It's pathetic and it's not feminine, in my opinion.

"There's the hospital," I tell Max. "Are you coming up with me? Or do you want me to get J.C.?"

"I'll come. If you have to translate anything to get him out, you two will be forever."

All about him. What took me so long to see that about Max? Maybe because when he liked me, he didn't act like this. At least, I don't remember him acting like this.

"For the record," Max mumbles, "you didn't seem very interested in seeing me when I picked you up, and I assumed since you made no effort, you dumped me."

I push a strand of loose hair over my ear, as if trying to ensure he said what I think he said. "Let me get this straight. I'm in a foreign country—your foreign country—and yet you didn't think I made enough of an effort? Did you expect me to propose?"

"I got nervous. Something about your attitude made me nervous."

"Which is not really my fault, right?"

"I thought you'd want to go out with your parents and me if you weren't ashamed of me."

"If that's the case, you don't seem very heartbroken. Is your heart broken or is your ego bruised?"

Max turns and stares at me, then back at the road before him. "Both, I suppose. The final insult being you thought of me only to pick up J.C., which means you never considered me a boyfriend. You didn't ask your parents, Claire—any of them could have rented a car to get your boyfriend to the airport and not messed up your mission work."

"There's a reason that I called you. I—"

"Did you want me to be jealous?" His eyes narrow as if he expects me to be guilty.

"What? No!"

"I see how it is now." Max grins like he's just finished a successful tango on *Dancing with the Stars*. He's got this aura of self-satisfaction that makes me want to slap the expression from his face. But then again, that only proves his point, as though I was trying to make him jealous, so I don't protest further.

"Max, I wouldn't wish that feeling on my worst enemy, so I can assure you, that was not part of my plan. You give me a lot of credit for planning ahead, and I'm not that organized. I called you because J.C. is pretty beat-up and he didn't want my parents to see him like that. He didn't want Libby to know the particulars for her safety—"

"Because you two were where you weren't supposed to be and you got caught?"

I sigh. "Because the man who hurt J.C. could hurt Libby if he found out J.C.'s connection."

Max exhales. "I knew it. This guy is going to be just like

Chase, no? He's got you believing he's saving everyone. The big hero, like Mr. Air Force Academy himself," he says, referring to my childhood crush.

"You are jealous."

Max opens his mouth to speak but shakes his head instead. "Never mind. Where are we picking this guy up? Do you have to check him out?"

"I thought I'd just go to his room and check his status."

The conversation is so shallow. Both of us want to avoid the real work of having an emotional conversation, I suppose. If Max was/is jealous, he's going to keep it to himself.

As we pull up to the hospital, Max drives into a parking spot and I notice J.C. seated on a red bench outside the building. I know it's now or never with Max. "Whether you did or didn't, I felt dumped by you and discarded on the side of the road."

"That's a bit dramatic, isn't it?"

"Maybe, but it's how I felt, and I thought you should know before you toss someone else aside. Girls have feelings, Max, and when you tell someone you love them, they expect it to show. All I'm saying." I reach for the door handle. "J.C.'s waiting. I'll be back with him."

Max tugs at my shoulder. "Daisy, wait."

I turn back toward him.

"I shouldn't have said I loved you."

I nod. "Consider it unsaid."

"Not because I didn't mean it. Because . . . it's complicated and I don't know how to say it."

J.C. rises from the bench as he sees me.

"It's all right. The explanation will probably hurt worse than the lack of one." I tug the door handle.

"I suppose you want me to help him limp to the car."

"Do whatever you'd like, Max." I push open the car door and hike my purse over my shoulder, though it has no money in it—that's still on my person. Still, it seems stupid to leave the bag in the car as a temptation for someone.

J.C. leans against the bench, a crutch under one arm. His blond hair is tousled, and he's got one eye still bandaged, a bruised, bulbous lip, and his left arm in a cast. "What are you doing here? I told you not to come so you didn't screw things up with Libby."

"I'm here. Let's leave it at that for now."

"That's Max?"

"Yeah."

"Decent of him to come."

"He thinks I invited him to make him jealous."

"Did you?"

I turn and cross my arms in front of me, forcing J.C. to stop walking. "Not you too! Did you not ask for Max?"

"Yeah, but since you're here, I have to wonder. Did you put your scholarship in jeopardy so you could make sure Max hadn't forgotten about you?"

I sigh. "Just get in the car. I'm done with guys. When I get home, I'm going to get my first cat. That's it. Just me and the cat. No guys to complicate my life. No one to make me feel inferior or stupid or accuse me of provoking people. Nope, from here on out, it's just the cat. They purr when they're happy, they screech when they're not. Very simple creatures, and clearly all my IQ can handle at this point."

"Someone got up on the wrong side of the bed," J.C. says. "Did you get kicked out of the mission?"

"Yes," I say as we start walking again.

"I knew it. She was just waiting for a reason. She doesn't know about Pablo or his stepfather, does she?"

"No, and let's just say keeping her safe was not the highest of my priorities when I left there."

"I don't have a free hand," he says, looking at one arm holding the crutch and the other in the cast. "But if I did, I'd applaud to tell you how proud I am of you."

"Save that thought. You might need to relay it to my parents via video chat when the swelling on your face disappears."

"What the heck happened to you?" Max asks him. "I'd shake your hand, but it looks like someone else has already shaken everything."

"Very funny. Thanks for coming to get me."

"When Daisy calls, I come running."

"Like when you were supposed to bring the candy to the mission?"

"I had to work."

"In America, we call our girlfriends when we can't show."

"Daisy didn't have a phone with her."

"You could have called the mission."

"Her parents told me not to, that she needed to concentrate on the work if she was going to get her paperwork signed. In my country, we honor thy parents."

"Yeah, well, in my—"

"Shut up! *Callate!*" I shout. "Both of you. What time's your flight, J.C.?"

"Three. I'm supposed to be there by one."

"That's only two hours from now!"

"That's plenty of time," he says. We pile into the car, and Max fires up the engine. He turns on the radio and we sit listening to the Latino polka-sounding music, each of us lost in our thoughts. As Max turns onto the highway, we drive past the mission and onto the high desert landscape that leads back to the city.

Max is focused on driving, and every once in a while he aims those gorgeous brown eyes at me in the rearview mirror. In the meantime, J.C. looks out the passenger window, and the three of us remain silent. No doubt each of us is thinking what an odd threesome we are and lacking the words to say what probably should be said.

I'm thinking about speaking when at that second there's an explosive sound in the car, as if a bomb has gone off. The car lurches to the side of the gravel road and hurtles toward a ditch. The short moment where the car is airborne feels eerily silent, and as I see the ditch rising to meet us, I brace myself against the front seat.

The car slams into a mound of dirt and pushes off to land in the ditch, where we come to a hard stop. The airbag deploys, and Max slumps over it. J.C. groans in agony, but otherwise the silence overwhelms us.

"Max?"

J.C. has hold of his own arm. "I think he's unconscious."

"Max!" I grab him from behind, wrap my arm around his shoulders, and lift his head off the steering wheel, then immediately realize I shouldn't have moved him. "Max!"

"His forehead is bleeding," J.C. says.

I hold Max's chin in my hand and he twists toward me. A wide grin spreads across his face.

"See, you like me best. You were worried."

"Aargh! You are exhausting! Your forehead's bleeding."

He presses his fingertips to his forehead and feels the gash, then brings his bloody fingers toward me. "I'm all right. Heads bleed a lot." He turns toward the windshield and the reality of our situation seems to hit him. "How are we going to get out of here?"

"What happened?"

"We had a blowout." Max uses a red rag to blot his forehead and presses against the cut to stop the bleeding. "I hope no one stole the spare tire out of the trunk lately."

"That's sick, dude," J.C. says, staring at the grease-stained rag.

"You should talk. If you hadn't passed on your luck to me, we wouldn't be in this mess." Max gets out of the car, and his gait doesn't look much more stable than J.C.'s. All of the windows are down in the heat, and the gravel road above us is free of any traffic. Or help. Max walks around the car on top of the ditch and surveys the damage. "We're stuck good. Your boyfriend isn't going to be able to help, so I think you have to get out, Daisy. We have to get the car back on the road before we can change the tire."

"Get out and do what?"

"Push. This car ain't going to move itself down here, and I need to change the tire."

"How long will that take?"

"Longer if you don't get out of the car quickly."

"I can help," J.C. offers and claws unsuccessfully at the door.

"J.C., just stay here. It's my day to be the hero. I'm a lot stronger than I look," I tell him.

He half grins. "I know that. I knew it before you did."

Max opens J.C.'s door, but it jams into the side of the ditch and he slams it shut again. "You have to try and steer.

Think you can manage that? The door won't open. You have to climb over there."

"Yeah," J.C. says with more bravado than I've heard from him before.

The ditch is not huge, more like a rut of three feet or so, but we're at the end of it, so we're going to have to push backwards before we can actually try to get out of the rut, and even then it's going to take a lot of momentum to push the tiny vehicle out of the ditch. The tire is shredded, with pieces of it littering the dirt road behind us.

"We're not going to make J.C.'s flight," I say.

"Thank you, Captain Obvious."

"Max! That was totally rude. I'm trying to help."

He exhales. "I'm sorry, but I'm going to be late for work, and now I have to pay for this tire. This is a sign I need a damsel with less distress."

"So you've told me. I'll pay for the dang tire, all right? I'm sorry I asked for your help. I won't do it again."

He picks up some of the shredded tire and tosses it back on the dirt in a puff of dust. "You'll pay for my tire so you can get your boyfriend to the airport on time?"

"Lower the drama, shall we? I'm not anyone's girlfriend. I'm not yours and I'm not his. I'm just a fired missionary with a mission to get friend number two back to Buenos Aires in friend number one's car so that the man who beat him up doesn't come after him again, and so that the missionary who hates me is safe from danger. Make sense?"

"Not a bit."

"Just push." I lean behind the car.

"Do you have it in neutral?" Max yells.

"Go!" J.C. yells out the window.

"One." Max looks at me from across the bumper, and there's just a glimmer of a smile on his face. "Two. Three. Push!"

I grunt and use everything I've got in my legs and hips, but the car goes nowhere.

"Sorry!" J.C. looks out the window. "Sorry, I thought it was in neutral, but I read it wrong. It's in neutral now!"

"Where did you find this guy?"

"It's probably different here. The markings on the car, I mean."

"*N* is the same in your language, no?"

"Can we just push?"

He does the count again and we push, and this time we get about halfway up the ditch before the car falls backwards and lands deeper than where it was originally.

"Maybe we can get a taxi and come back for the car?"

"Daisy, do you know what would happen if you left your car back home on the east side of town overnight?"

"It would be pieced out and sold as parts by the next morning?"

"Exactly. This may not be much, but it's all I've got, so we're not leaving it here."

"I have my mom's cell phone. Do you have Triple A or whatever the equivalent is here?"

"I'm going to ignore that question. You ready to push? Or have you solved it all now?"

I stick my tongue out at him. "I'm ready."

"After we push and the car rolls, let it come all the way back and then we'll use the downward motion to push again. Got it?"

"I took physics."

"Just not geography that tells you you're not in America and the tow truck will be along any second now."

"There are tow trucks in Argentina, Max. You make me sound ignorant."

"There are. Just not here and just not any I can afford."

"I can call a taxi for J.C. and me." I realize how incredibly selfish that sounds the minute I say it.

"All right, let's go!" J.C. yells out the window.

Max holds his arm out as if to say "go ahead." I keep my eyes focused on Max but speak to J.C. "We're not leaving without Max."

J.C. eyes me and follows my gaze. I can see him out of the corner of my eye, and we both know I'm not as over Max as I'd like to be. Why do I have to be so fiercely loyal? Max lives halfway across the world. J.C. is going to my college. Max has commitment issues. J.C. lets a girl know when it's over.

I wish I was like my mother and could love practically. I swear, my life would be ten times easier.

~13~

Max counts to three again, and we heave the car slightly up the small hill. It rolls back, and we rush out of the way and break into laughter, even though the car is farther in the rut than when we started this process.

"That didn't work," I say. "Maybe J.C. should get out. The extra weight can't help."

Max shoots me a look. "He needs to put on the brake when we get it to the top of the ditch or we'll roll back down again. Come on, again. One, two, three!"

We grunt and strain and end up with the two left tires on the road, and J.C. jams the car into park and tightens the emergency brake. How he did that without full use of his limbs I'll never understand, but we've made progress, and the three of us smile.

"Now what?" I ask.

"Let me think a minute," Max says, his thumb and bent forefinger rubbing at his chin.

J.C. leans out the car's window. "If I get the car turned to the left, do you think you two can make one more go of it?"

Max and I look at each other, and our eyes linger in the decision. "We can try," he says.

A beat-up truck barrels down the road, drives beyond us, and pulls to the side. Two guys wearing jeans and cowboy hats jump out, and I don't know whether to be happy we've been rescued or anxious that we're all out in the middle of nowhere. The two guys slam the truck's doors and approach the car. The closer they get, the more the idea they're here to help gives way to anxiety that we're so vulnerable.

The two men are slender and tan though it's the middle of winter, and they too look like they belong in a boy band. With the exception that this is a rougher band. Maybe they're playing bars at night and spitting out chewing tobacco before the performance. I'd say they appear to be in their late twenties. I don't know what they're feeding the guys down here—maybe it's an extra dose of sunshine or the southern hemisphere's exposure—but we seriously need to import some to America. It's better than any antiaging crème Nordstrom is selling.

The two men say something in Spanish to Max, and all I can make out is *car* and *yes* from Max, but I watch the exchange closely to see if I should still be more fearful than relieved.

"*Hola*," one of the guys says to me and tips his hat. I'm telling you, I am Scarlett Johansson down here. I'm never going back. It's settled. It's not me. It's the guys of America. My rejection here was short-lived. Now my dance card is full.

"*Hola*," I say back.

"Get out of the way, Daisy," Max shouts at me, as though I've offended him somehow. "We're going to push the car the rest of the way out."

I stand to the field side of the rut and let the guys take over.

I brush my hands off, glad to be done with manual labor for the day. "I'm so hungry," I grumble. "I can't wait to get to town, and I'm going to eat a massive Argentine steak."

No one's listening to me, but that hardly affects me. I'm just happy that the country is full of strapping men ready to do the hard labor and get me to the spa as soon as possible. The fact is, if you're going to fail at mission work, there are worse ways to go.

Max shouts at J.C. to let the brake go, and the three guys heave the car onto the road with one swift push. Max didn't even count.

I clap. "Yay! Now we just need to change the tire and we're on our way to town!"

The two good Samaritans open the trunk without a word, whisk out the tools, and toss them on the road with a clang. They pull up the pathetic spare tire that doesn't look like it has enough legs to get us to the next town, much less Buenos Aires, but I keep my mouth shut. Max is already irritated beyond belief at me, and his pointed glares make no secret of the idea. In a few hours I'll never have to see him again, I remind myself.

J.C. hobbles out of the car, his blond hair and tan skin looking remarkably Californian for a guy from Arizona. He limps over to see if he can help the guys, but they act as if they can't understand his Spanish. Max shoos him off with a brush of his fingers. I may not know a lot about guys, but that's the ultimate dis. To emasculate a guy like he can't change a tire, in front of a woman, is not cool. Truthfully, I don't know if J.C. or Max can change a tire, but I know man-speak for "go away," and that was it.

I tap my foot, convinced there's nothing more I can do

until we're back on the road, when my job will be getting J.C. off into the wild blue yonder and getting myself a carnivorous meal.

J.C. has his backpack with him, and he pulls out a bottled soda. "You thirsty?" he asks me. "You don't want to get dehydrated out here. I know it doesn't feel warm, but you're not used to the atmosphere."

"Do you carry a grocery store in that thing?" I raise my brows at Mr. Boy Scout, who seems to be ready for anything.

"Apple?" He holds out a piece of green fruit, and I take it from him. His hand brushes mine, and it forces my eyes to his.

"Thank you."

"I've got an extra candy bar too. You want one?"

"No thanks." I take a bite from the apple.

"Sorry I made things uncomfortable for you and Max. I didn't think about that aspect of it."

"I did that all by myself. I shouldn't have come down here in the first place. He probably felt stalked, and clearly the mission didn't go as planned. Claire and I should have gone to Hawaii like every other graduating senior on a trip."

"Then you wouldn't have met me," he says with a warm smile.

"You're right."

We hear a loud clang and look up to see the car buzzing away from us, the tools left in a heap next to the old tire's remains. Max is on the ground at the bottom of the ditch.

"What happened?" I ask.

"My car!" Max wails with his hands in the air. "My car!" His hands grip his head, then raise to the sky again. He starts to speak rapidly in Spanish, and J.C. and I stare at each other in disbelief.

"Did his car just get stolen?" I ask J.C. "He's going to kill me."

"I guess God doesn't want me to get home." J.C. shrugs, and I do wish I could have his attitude.

"All my stuff was in there!" I say, promptly realizing my selfishness when Max comes toward me wielding Spanish words like verbal swords. He's waving his arms to punctuate the jabs. "Max, I'm sorry. I'm so sorry! I don't know what to say." I look past him and see the tail end of his car disappearing along the beaten road. "We can take their truck!" I point to the jalopy slumped on the side of the road.

"You don't think there's a reason they took my car?" Max stares at the truck. It's obvious he has no faith in its ability to get us anywhere.

"Just to the next town until we can call the police. What choice do we have?"

"Do you have your wallets on you at least?"

J.C. and I nod.

"Passports?"

"Yeah," we both answer.

"Let's take the truck. We don't have much choice," Max says, but I feel guilt to my toes. He turns to me. "And you. You were flirting with the guys who stole my car!"

"Max, you don't have to blame me for everything that's gone wrong. I get it, all right? And I wasn't flirting, I said '*hola*.' The only Spanish word I know with confidence, besides *bathroom*, which didn't seem appropriate for the moment."

"It was the way you said *hola*."

"In other words, the way I said *hola* invited them to steal the car. Don't you think they meant to steal the car in the first place or they wouldn't have stopped?"

He pauses at this, and I'm grateful for the reprieve. I don't know if he's jealous or, as J.C. indicated, just an all-around jerk, but I'm beginning to think the latter.

"Just let me think a minute," Max snaps.

"Cut it out!" J.C. hobbles on his crutch with his backpack heaved over the shoulder of his broken arm. "If you want to yell at someone, yell at me. Daisy's not even supposed to be here, and she wouldn't be if Libby were any kind of decent person. She's taken enough on this trip, and if you can't be kind to her, just get out of the way. Didn't your mother teach you how to treat a lady?" he snipes. "Did it ever occur to you that those guys could have hurt her? Quit thinking about yourself and get us to the next town. I'll take care of your stupid car! I'm sorry I involved either one of you in this mess, but blame the right person."

"That stupid car is how I earn my living," Max says. "It's how I get elderly people where they need to go to buy food and medicine. It's not a joyride, okay?"

"I said I'd take care of it. Apologize to Daisy!" J.C.'s voice leaves little room for argument, and even though he's beat to heck, his tone invokes respect.

"I'm sorry, Daisy. I'm going to be late, and I hadn't planned on any of this. There are people back home counting on me."

"Shouldn't we call the police about the car?" I take out my parents' cell phone, grateful I kept it in my pocket and not in my handbag, which is long gone. "You could call your friends, Max."

"My friends don't have a cell phone. And put that away before it gets stolen as well. I know where the police station is in the next town. Just get in the truck and let's pray it starts." Max runs ahead, but I stay back to walk with J.C.

"Everything I touch turns to disaster."

J.C. stops walking and leans on his crutch. "Maybe it's not you. I prayed this morning that I'd have more time with you. Who am I to question how God gives it to me?"

"Are you for real?"

"I felt called down here, and for what? To get stung by a scorpion, beaten by a thug, and rejected by my mission field? I have to think God had something in mind when he called me down here. You can look at all the negatives, or you can look at the fact that I'm walking along a country road with the most beautiful girl, inside and out."

"I have never met anyone quite like you, J.C."

Up ahead, we hear Max fire up the truck, and we can be grateful for that. J.C. smiles at the sound of the engine, and I help him climb into the cab of the truck. He slyly takes my hand in his own while Max lets the hand brake go and pushes the crank into gear. We're rumbling toward town when the sounds of sirens pierce our ears. Behind us are several police cars with lights flashing. Max pulls the truck over to the side again.

"I don't think you're going to make your plane," I say to J.C. I'll admit, I said it so he'd look at me with those luscious gray-green eyes.

"I'll call my grandmother when we get into town." J.C. turns and looks at the police cars (three of them) behind us. "If we make it to town."

Max is looking in his rearview mirror, or whoever's rearview mirror this is, and I clutch J.C.'s hand tighter and feel a pulse of electricity shoot up my arm.

"My mom's going to kill me!" I say.

How on earth did I get here? And why? Why do I always get myself into these situations? I must look into this pattern. I just hope I'll have the time and not be stuck in an Argentine jail.

14

My Life: Stop—July 9

My travel journal was stolen with my stuff, so I'm writing on scrap paper. I was tempted to use my passport, since I doubt it will get much more in the way of stamps, but I refrained. Clearly all the hope hasn't gone out of me yet.

Factoid: Too much optimism can render you unprepared to handle life's traumas. That's not my issue, though I am feeling unprepared for today's traumas.

Life seems to be one step forward, two steps backward:

1. Meet a guy who is not afraid to share his feelings and always has food close by.

A. Max is here making me question if any guy will ever actually like me for me.

B. Since I'm going to be late, my parents will never, ever trust me again to date until I'm at least thirty.

2. Find a way to get J.C. to the airport on time and not let Libby be blamed for Pablo's disappearance by Child Protective Services.

A. Max's car is stolen.

B. The truck we managed to pick up was used in a bank robbery. We spent all afternoon being questioned for a federal crime and are now involved in an international incident. The American embassy (and my parents) have been notified. I am going to be grounded until my deathbed.

I never thought I'd write this: I know what the inside of an Argentine jail looks like! Granted, I didn't have to actually stay in one, and all I can say is thank GOODNESS that Max was along for translation because I don't know that J.C., with his blond good looks and spotty Spanish, would have gotten us out of trouble.

Max explained our story, and eventually it checked out, thanks to a few phone calls to the American embassy. But Max's car is officially gone.

We sit outside this one-horse town discussing our options, since my parents were not at the hotel and will arrive to notification from the American embassy. Ah, I wonder what the lucky people are doing today.

"How long are you going to write on garbage?" Max asks me. "The police said we're free to go. It doesn't look like my car is showing up anytime soon, so we might as well get back to town. Do you have money for a cab?"

"You know, you were a lot nicer in America." I shove the scrap of paper into the passport pouch I have around my neck and put it under my shirt again. "I was just going to describe the police station. My adventure with the law in Argentina. Maybe I can use it for a paper when I get to Pepperdine."

"If we get to Pepperdine," J.C. says. "At this rate, we'll be lucky to get back to America."

"That doesn't sound like you, J.C."

"My leg hurts and all my pain meds were attached to my bedroll."

"I don't see why you have to write it down. This isn't the first time you've been to the police station." Max seems to say this for J.C.'s benefit.

J.C. stares at me and I feel the need to explain. "I had a stalker in high school. Claire's older half brother. I just had to go to the station and explain because it was sort of a kidnapping. Like today, you know? The police just wanted to check out my story."

"The point is, to have two run-ins with the law when you go to a Christian high school—wait a minute, the party you had in high school." Max points at me. "Three! Three run-ins with the law! I should have known your visit would end in trouble for me."

"I'm bad luck, I get it."

J.C. starts to laugh. "Look at me. I think we were made for each other." He kisses me on the cheek.

Max stands up abruptly. "If you two want to spend your life trying to stay alive, you need to leave me out of it. Bonnie and Clyde didn't need a third wheel. I'll hitch a ride back to town."

"Don't be stupid. We have to call a taxi for us anyway."

"I can call a friend to pick me up," Max says.

"You? But not us, is that what you're saying?" I ask him. "You've turned into quite the villain, Max. You're taking on a *Count of Monte Cristo* revenge persona."

"Is that what you think?" Max asks. "You're certain it's me then? That you didn't betray me with my archenemy, *Mercedes*?"

"I wouldn't leave you in an American police station if you didn't speak the language, that's for sure. Look at what J.C. did with Libby, who never gave him a decent word. He put himself on the line for a child, and for Libby. I didn't think I was expecting a lot to ask for your help. I would have helped you if this situation were reversed."

"Well, then he's the hero of this story. You've already implied that."

Max's hurt expression gets to me. I'm such a sucker for the underdog. Even if he made himself the underdog!

"Max, you made it clear you were leaving America, and that was that. It's just your ego that's bruised. Admit that much, won't you? If I meant something to you, you would have moved heaven and earth to pick me up for dinner when I got here."

He doesn't address any of this. "All right. You two are welcome in my friend's car. I'll call her now."

"Her?" I ask with raised eyebrows.

"Are you jealous?" J.C. asks me.

I clear my throat. "No, I'm not jealous, but he shouldn't be railing on me if he's got another girl on the side. All I'm sayin'."

"I'm going to call my friend now. This is beyond awkward." Max walks away from us.

"What are you going to do about the mission requirement for school?" J.C. asks me.

I shrug. "The truth is, I haven't thought about it. Not until I told my parents my plan. I guess pray for the best and hope they don't have someone lined up behind us to take our places. I can't afford Pepperdine without the scholarship. You?"

"I can still make it up at home at the food bank." J.C.'s voice is somber. "But it doesn't look good that neither one of us finished the ministry we signed up for. Hope they allow the switch. It ticks me off I won't have that international experience on my résumé, though."

"Yeah. Me too. But I'd be happy to vouch for you. To tell them how you protected Libby, even if she didn't know what you did." I lift my hair off the back of my neck, wishing for a shower. "Somehow, losing my mission requirement—what I feared most—doesn't seem that bad now that it's gone."

"Yeah." J.C.'s tone doesn't agree with his answer.

"I imagine they'll look at our ministry histories and take them into account."

"You would think so."

"Still, I'm proud of you for what you did. It takes a lot to do so much for a person who won't even appreciate it or know what you did for them."

Max has walked back to our pity party and doesn't seem to empathize. "If you two are done with your mutual fan club, my friend is coming. Should be here in about twenty minutes."

"We're only that far from Buenos Aires?"

"Not even that far."

"We could have taken a cab."

"My point exactly," Max comments, but I ignore his meaning. He ditched me. I'm not going to feel guilty about asking a favor when I'm in his country.

"Well, we have to look at the silver lining, right? I'm so grateful that Claire freaked about me keeping my money on my body. All my stuff is gone except for the money and my passport."

"It's all you need. You can get new clothes in town," J.C. says. "My stuff . . . I hope they need it more than I did, that's all I can say. At least you kept your jacket on."

"Let's hope my mom won't find a sewing machine and whip me up something while we're down here." I laugh at this, but no one seems to get it and I laugh alone. Claire would have totally appreciated the humor.

Suddenly I feel alone. Very alone. I'm trying to think of some sort of stimulating conversation to fill the awkward silence, but I've got nothing.

"Was this worth it?" Max asks me.

"Was it worth you losing your car?" I shake my head. "No. I feel horrible, Max. I just didn't want anyone to get hurt." I glance at J.C. and all his bandages. "Hurt worse, I mean."

Max aims those deep brown eyes straight at me with the first real eye contact he's given me since I arrived. "You did the right thing. We don't always get rewarded for doing the right thing."

"I know. It sucks."

"I agree," J.C. says. "Life should be fair. I guess we all do what we can to make life as fair as we can."

"Only Americans think that. Other countries seem to know instinctively that life isn't fair. You grow up watching children not have enough food to eat in your neighborhood, and you get that life isn't fair. What did they ever do to anyone? Sin enters the world, and we all get to witness it in one way or another. J.C. here, he gets to *feel* it," Max says in reference to J.C.'s bandages.

"We know life's not fair. In America, we do our level best to make it fair because that's what's right."

"Yeah, sure," Max answers.

I watch as the two guys have this invisible but palpable war going on between them to be deemed right. I'd like to believe it's about me, but ultimately I think it's about the male ego.

"I'm going to *el baño* before we have to leave." J.C. gets up on one leg by balancing and hobbles into the police station again.

Max's expression softens, and since I've been here, this is the first time I've seen the Max I thought I knew in America. Sure, he's been charming, but not really present. Not where I felt like he was really beside me in the moment, and it brings an air of intimacy that makes me slightly uncomfortable without J.C. there.

"I'm sorry," he says.

"Sorry?"

"I have to stay here. In Argentina. My mom is sick and there's no one to help but me. So college is probably out of the question for right now."

"I thought you planned to go to school here all along."

"I didn't have a choice, but watching the two of you about to go off and get educated while falling for each other doesn't exactly help my attitude."

"I don't understand. Are you trying to say something to me that I'm supposed to be reading? Because my brain doesn't really work on that level. I need you to just say it."

"I was harsh with you . . . you know, silent, because—"

"Wait a minute." I stop him with my hand held up. "You were ignoring me on purpose?" Because here I thought I'd only imagined the dis, but come to find out it was real and, worse yet, planned.

"Let me explain. I—"

J.C. walks out and stands between us. "They don't have a public restroom. Isn't the police station a public building, so by all rights and standards, shouldn't the restroom be public?"

I open my mouth to speak, but nothing comes out. I just want to know what Max had to say. I want to know if he really didn't want to dump me but did it for some self-sacrificial reason, because let's face it, that would be totally hot.

Max glares at J.C., who picks up on it immediately. "Did I interrupt something?"

"If you don't mind, I'd like to talk to Daisy alone for a minute."

"Daisy, you all right with that?" J.C. asks in that chivalrous way I've grown so fond of in a few short days.

"Sure."

I'd like to be a romantic and say that Max's explanation is at the top of my list of priorities, but really all I can think about right now is my future at Pepperdine, and how I'm going to explain to my parents that I need to change my flight home . . . or that when they finally decided to trust me, I ended up alone with two guys in a Podunk town outside of a jail without transportation. That one's not going to look good on a daughter résumé.

A car pulls up and Max's expression falls. "That's our ride."

This conversation is never going to happen, so in my mind, I'm just going to pretend that he pronounces he did love me but circumstances make our being together impossible. That's far more romantic than whatever reality may have to offer me.

15

Max, J.C., and I sit in awkward silence until the car pulls up to the police station. The vehicle is a black stretch town car of some sort, with international diplomacy plates.

"I thought we were done with the embassy."

"It's my friend," Max says without further explanation.

He opens the massive car door and bends in to offer some kind of explanation about J.C. and me. Then he motions for us to get into the vehicle. I help J.C. off the wood porch of the police station and we head to the car, grateful our excursion is finally over for the day.

Max opens the back door and we slide in. "Hi," I say.

The driver turns toward me. She is gorgeous—petite, dark, and exotic features with a model's high cheekbones and facial structure. Her hands are so tiny and delicate that I feel like a horse sliding in the backseat. Her presence makes me decide that Max's flirtation with me was just that—a flirtation. His feelings never went where mine did, and obviously I was too infatuated to see any of it.

She's still fixated on Max outside the car, and the way she looks at him, as if she's more than thrilled he called her, tells me my romantic views of life can last only so long and then reality must take its place.

Two men. Two gorgeous guys were not in love with me. I only imagined their feelings because mine were so strong. Now I want to go running back to my mommy and Claire, and I promise myself that I will listen to their truth. No matter how difficult it is to hear, it's better than getting my heart broken time and time again.

The petite princess finally acknowledges my presence. The girl lets her wrist dangle over the seat and offers a limp handshake. "Rosalina," she says. "I assume you're Daisy?" Her English is perfect with only a hint of an accent, which makes her all the more exotic and sexy.

I nod. "This is J.C."

She reaches her tiny hand to J.C. and greets him equally.

Rather than being a woman with two guys aching for her love—competing for it, in essence—in reality, I am a girl who barely avoided jail, flunked a missionary project needed for college admission, and let down her parents, all in one fell swoop. No one can say I'm not efficient.

"So you are Daisy. The infamous Daisy."

I nod again. "You know me?" Point, Max's hot chick.

She glances at Max and it's not a kind look. "I've heard about you."

"So you're going to sit in the back?" Rosalina says as though she is not happy about the situation. "Am I to be your chauffeur?"

"J.C. needs to stretch out his leg. I think he should come up front," Max says, eyeing me to let J.C. out of the car. "Relax, Rosa."

"I had to get out of work to pick you all up."

"We really appreciate it," I tell her. "Max was so kind to come and get J.C. so there would be no more trouble at the mission, and he got paid back by having his car stolen. It's really awful."

"I'll bet. How will you work now, Max?" Rosalina asks him. "Can't save for a ring without a job, can you?"

I flinch at her words. Save for a ring? I stare at Max to see his startled expression, but it isn't there. He's as calm as can be. I, however, am about ready to go postal. *You want to answer her, Romeo?* my look asks him.

"I'll figure it out."

"You'll what?" I ask, but his harsh eyes ask for a favor, and I take the pressure off the situation. "So, how do you two know each other?"

"Max is my boyfriend. Soon to be my fiancé. Or didn't he tell you?" She flips her long, dark hair around and faces me with her deep brown eyes, a look I'm certain would throw daggers if she were capable of a superpower.

"Fiancé? Aren't you two a little young to be thinking of marriage?"

"Our mothers have been thinking of nothing else since we were babies. We were destined for one another. Isn't that right, Max?" Rosalina coos.

Max doesn't answer, and as J.C. slips into the front seat, it occurs to me that while I didn't have the right to date, maybe Max never did either. Only his reasons were far darker than my own. It never occurred to me that I wasn't the problem.

I struggle to find my happy voice, but the first sound is nothing more than a squawk. "Have you two been together long?"

"Since before he left for America, officially, but unofficially, since we were babies. His father made him go, you know, and I thought it was going to be an international battle to get him back. To help his father with that ridiculous hot dog stand in the mall when his mother needed him. When he could have just hired some American idiot. The man knew Max's mother needed him here. I can't stand how selfish that was, but he's back now." She licks her lips when she glances at Max.

"You speak such good English," I tell her, trying to avoid my own feelings about Max being forced to come back to Argentina against his will.

"My mother is the American ambassador—that's how she met my father. It's also how I knew where Max was before he called me. I work at the embassy coordinating NGOs. Right now I'm working on an upcoming fair to get more foreign-aid workers into the country. Nongovernmental organizations that help with the country's needs, you understand?"

"Wow, that's impressive," I say honestly. "Do any of these NGOs have need of some American help for the next week?"

"Because?"

"I have to do some charitable work, preferably in another country, for my scholarship at Pepperdine University, and unfortunately I didn't really mesh with the mission where I was."

"Because you acted like a spoiled American? Max told me all about the spoiled Americans he dealt with when in your country."

"Rosalina! Daisy's my friend—haven't you known me to always choose my friends well?" Max asks. "I assure you that she's no spoiled American."

"I've known you to always choose them pretty, I'll say that

much for you. But once we're married, you'll have to tone that down. I can be very jealous, you know."

"That's so sweet, Rosalina, but wow, I can only wish I were one-tenth as exotic and beautiful as you. Max definitely had to lower his standards in America. I think I have yet to meet someone in this country who couldn't be a movie star in America." I hope to soften her dislike of me and find myself a ministry quickly that qualifies for Pepperdine without me having to go home and find something mundane and domestic that won't look nearly as impressive on my résumé.

I can see her grin in the rearview mirror, and it's not like I was dishonest, but I'm shocked at how well she takes my compliment. She's actually beaming a smile with her perfect white teeth and her full, naturally red lips.

"I think it's the healthy lifestyle. It's a city lifestyle, but also very close to the earth. We have the best of Europe and Latin America here, and I think it shows in the people."

"I wouldn't doubt it, it obviously agrees with you all."

The tension in the car is so thick, it almost makes me wish for the freedom of the side of the road without a vehicle.

"So you never dated Max?" Rosalina asks. "Is that what you're trying to make me believe?"

Max turns and glares at me, as if I was ever tempted to tell Rosalina I dated her future husband. Something tells me she has henchmen lying in wait.

"Max had one pity dance with me at the prom. He was so sweet to do that. I had to work the Breathalyzer machine at the dance—"

"You have a Breathalyzer machine at your high school? The teachers can't tell if a person is drunk or not? Does anyone actually show up that way?"

"It's just a precaution," I tell her.

"Did you find my future fiancé to be a good dancer?"

"I did."

The car seems to float in slow motion as we make our way toward the city, and I wish I could beam out of this uncomfortable situation.

"Max, you were telling me the truth?" She stares across the car and flutters her eyelashes, all while following frighteningly close to the car in front of her. "I thought for certain he'd taken an American girl for a spin. We hear a lot about your reputations."

"Um, car. Car up there," I say to divert Rosa's attentions from Max to driving. "Won't do us any good to earn a ring if we're not alive to get it, will it?"

"You were saying, American girl?"

It takes everything I have not to retort with some smart-aleck comment about the easy ways of South America, but that will get me nowhere with the mission work, not to mention I don't even know if it's true.

"You can't believe everything you hear, or acknowledge Americans by the garbage Hollywood puts out. I went to a strict Christian school, and we were expected to behave accordingly."

"That's good to hear. Max can be so charming, you know. I wouldn't blame an American girl for wanting to come back with him and be Argentine. I thought he might want to sow his wild oats while he was there in America."

"This car ride is actually the first time my parents have approved of me being alone with a boy. Never even had a date, so if you had something to worry about with Max, it certainly wasn't with me."

She offers Max a warm smile and turns back to the road. "So what hotel are you staying at?"

"In Recoleta, at the Palace Alvear. Is there any way we can make it to the airport before your flight?" I say to J.C.

"Hmmm," she says. "No way on the airport." J.C.'s shoulders deflate. "So, rich parents, huh? Recoleta?"

"Not mine. My best friend's rich parents."

"Where is she? Back at the hotel?"

"She's still at the mission to finish out the week. The woman in charge liked her, but I seemed to set her nerves on edge."

"Because you're pretty, no doubt." Rosa's compliment made me uneasy, as if the other shoe would drop soon.

"I'm nothing special in America. Claire is prettier."

"She isn't!" Both Max and J.C. say this, and for once I wish they hadn't come to my rescue. I feel it as Rosalina punches the gas pedal.

"So about that nongovernmental agency work . . ." I try to change the subject.

"Really, you're considered, I don't know, average in America?"

"Daisy isn't considered average anywhere," J.C. says. "She put her entire future on the line to do what's right and protect someone who, quite frankly, didn't deserve protecting." He turns and sets his chin on his good arm over the front seat. "With all I've endured down here, I can't imagine not knowing her now."

"You seem awfully invested in Daisy. How long have you two known each other?"

"We met three days ago, but I've seen her character in action and I know a good person when I meet one." He reaches over the seat and grabs my hand. In my peripheral vision I see Max roll his eyes.

"So you're recommending her for a position if I can find one quickly?" Rosalina asks.

"Absolutely I am. My only wish is that I weren't crippled so that I could stay and do the ministry alongside her."

"How'd that happen?"

"First I got stung by a scorpion. Then I got a pounding for turning in a child abuser."

"Max, what do you have to say to all this?" Rosalina asks. "Do you want Daisy to stay in the country and get her scholarship requirement?"

Max pauses, and it's obvious he needs to tread carefully, but I'm praying he'll come through for me.

"This whole trip has been surreal."

Everyone looks at me.

"Did I say that out loud?" I ask.

Rosalina begins to laugh. "Is she for real?"

"She is," Max says firmly. "One hundred percent genuine."

"Max?" Rosalina's voice softens. "Does that mean you want her to stay?"

"Of course I want her to stay. Her college career is at stake, and she worked hard for that. I have no doubt she'd get another scholarship, but not like this, and it wouldn't be as good this late in the summer. If it's in your power to offer something to her, I'd say if I mean anything to you, my friend's predicament will mean something to you."

"Your friend? Or the girl who kept you company while you were in the States?"

"This is ridiculous," I say. "I need this ministry, and if you need volunteers now, don't let jealousy—unfounded jealousy, I might add—get in your way."

"Daisy, do yourself a favor and just go chill at the fancy

hotel with your parents, and hang with Claire when she gets back," Max says. "You'll be fine. Things always work out fine for you, and I'm sure this time will be no different. Like a cat, you always land on your feet."

"But . . ."

The car is silent for the next fifteen minutes or so. As we pull into the outskirts of Buenos Aires, the luxurious, European-style buildings with their decorative fronts beam at us, and while I'm excited to tour the city, I'm also weary of this trip and ready to go home to my toilet-paper infused bedroom.

Finally Rosalina speaks up. "I have the perfect job for you, Daisy, and if you promise to cut off all communication with Max in the future, then I think it's for you. Do you think you could start tomorrow?"

"I can start right now!" I say excitedly.

Max is sulking next to me, and I'm torn about how I feel about him. I mean, never in the amount of time I spent with him did I hear Rosalina's name mentioned. Not even once. At the same time, my parents are so into courting and not dating, and I thought that was a fate worse than death, until I think about being engaged to someone who is lovely but not necessarily lovable, and certainly not Max's choice.

He conveys something to me with his eyes, and instinctively I understand that there is more to this offer than Rosalina is conveying.

"There's a manila folder back there marked 'United Nations.' It's a job taking census information on the population—more specifically, working with young pregnant women. I think you'd be perfect for the job. The young women would trust you immediately, I'll bet."

"Why do you say that?"

"Just being an American. We have our preconceived ideas, I guess you'd say."

My desperation speaks for me. To go back to the States with my paperwork signed trumps anything that Rosalina could do to me. "I'll take it!"

"How's your Spanish?"

"I read it better than I speak it, but if I have the questions written down, I'm sure I can speak well enough to get all the information the agency needs and be effective."

"What if they answer you in a long Spanish sentence? What then?" Max asks.

"I'll tell them *muy rapido*—it's too fast—and I'll get this really confused look on my face." I show Rosalina my best confused look and she nods.

"Then it's yours. Take the folder and review it as we get into town. The address is there on the folder, and you can just take a taxi to it in the morning. I'll call them and tell them to expect you. They'll be so excited. It was the one position we couldn't fill."

I try not to hear the warning bells in my head caused by this statement. It's far too convenient that a mission would appear right when I needed it. There has to be a catch.

Max crosses his arms as if he's been betrayed by me, but if you ask me, he's getting exactly what he deserves. Maybe losing the car was a bit much, but does he expect me to turn down an opportunity because of his own issues?

"He's engaged," I mumble under my breath. Only J.C. seems to notice my momentary absence as the full weight of this phrase hits me. I plaster on a smile to let him know I'm fine. No big deal. I glance at Max and see the late afternoon sun warming his tan skin through the window. His appearance is so *Tiger Beat*, and I wish staring at him didn't make my stomach do somersaults. I always knew something stopped Max from getting too close to me, but he allowed me to believe there was something wrong with me. Or I guess I allowed myself to believe that. Now I know he was settled on a wife and a future in this country. Any words to the contrary were just that—words. I see only disaster ahead for him if he goes through with his mother's wishes, but it's none of my business.

Max catches me staring, and I snap my head down to open the manila folder. The project's objectives are all in both English and Spanish, so I have no trouble reading about the requirements.

I feel J.C. staring at me, and I look up to see his questioning eyes. *He knows.* There's an invisible connection between Max and me, and it's as if I can read his heart. I trust him, even though maybe I shouldn't.

Everything about J.C. screams that he's perfect for me. He's unattached. Gorgeous. Sweet. Kind. He's going to be attending Pepperdine. He rescued me and stood up for me against Max's false accusations, and he's such a gentleman! Granted, maybe he has my luck and the two of us could be dangerous together, but other than that . . .

I feel my gaze stray back to Max, whom I should be livid with, but I can't stir up any anger for him again. He probably had no more control over his situation than I did about not being able to date. He can't want this. At my church, I've never seen any guy in a rush to get down the aisle.

But that invisible connection that goes against all the practicality and wisdom that I've gained in my short seventeen

16

The awkward silence stretches until J.C. casually mentions the weather, the palm trees we pass, and the Disneyland architecture. The car slows as we enter city traffic, pass through a huge roundabout, and crawl through several lanes. We head into the heart of the international world that I'm both in awe of and mesmerized by. The buzz of cars and people fills me with an energy of safety and sanity. Seeing familiar brands along many of the storefronts is solace enough to soothe me and make me feel as if I've entered society again. We've all fallen silent again as we check out the sights.

Rosalina speaks, pointing to the light-up clock in the center of the dashboard. "It looks like J.C. already missed his flight, so I'll drop you both off at the hotel." Rosalina doesn't mince words that she means J.C. and me. "Max, I'll get you back to your mother's. She's got to be worried sick about you. Wait until she hears about the car."

"Why do you think I didn't call her? I can wait for that conversation."

J.C. throws me a glance, and I do my best not to return it, in case Max sees and knows exactly what I'm thinking. But the closer we get to the hotel, the more I think I'll never see

Max again. I feel the sting of tears behind my nose at the very thought of this.

Max needs to stand up for himself. He needs to tell this control freak he's not getting married, and he needs to tell his mother that he has to choose his own life path. Otherwise his life will be constantly dictated for him from here on out. I know that it's none of my business, but that doesn't stop my body from buzzing with the stress of his situation.

As Rosalina pulls the oversized black car into the hotel's circular driveway, I feel my pulse quicken and hear my own heartbeat over the city sounds. She pulls the car toward the top of the circle and away from the bellmen, but they run alongside the car to ensure they can do their jobs and open the car doors. For seventeen, Rosalina looks and acts about thirty, and she intimidates me. It's clear she intimidates Max too. Besides, nice guys are no match for conniving women. I feel a sense of duty to be his heroine.

One of the bellmen opens the back door first, and Max climbs out. I follow quickly behind him to try for a few stealth moments of communication. We stand by the car, out of Rosalina's view.

"I might never see you again." I'd hoped to keep the desperation out of my voice, but I'm not so lucky.

"Would that bother you?"

"It would."

"How much?"

I've got nothing to lose here. My dignity left a long time ago. "I can't explain why I feel connected to you, like even though sometimes I don't get your actions, I trust who you are on the inside. I can't explain why I feel disappointed every time you don't show up, even though I knew you probably wouldn't. Still, it stings when you don't."

"Max!" Rosalina calls from the car. "J.C. is waiting to get out. What's going on out there?"

Max halts me with his eyes. "Please don't do this work for Rosalina." His eyes rest on the manila envelope.

"I promised Rosalina. Just like you did."

"Daisy, I had to say that. Rosalina is—she has this skill to get her way. It's best to agree with her, but you're not staying, so you don't need to do that."

"You lied when you urged me to take the mission?"

"I didn't lie. I encouraged you in front of Rosalina, and now I'm discouraging you when she can't hear me," he whispered, but he seemed rushed.

"Don't forget J.C. up here!" Rosalina calls. "What are you two talking about out there?" She can't see us, and being left out obviously doesn't sit well with her.

I lean into the car. "Got him. Be right there, J.C. Max and I are just working out how I'll get to the mission this week." I pop back up and meet Max's eyes again. "I promised," I say again, and before I have time to think of it, I ask him straight up. "Have you asked her to marry you? Is there a ring?"

He shakes his head and skirts a fuller answer. "I wonder how God feels about your promise. About promising something you're not capable of understanding."

"I told you, I have enough Spanish to listen to the questions."

"I never saw Rosa do an act of kindness that didn't have an ulterior motive attached to it."

"That's not a very nice way to think about your fiancée."

"She's not my fiancée. Those words came out of my mother's mouth, not mine. It's complicated. My mom works for Rosa's mom. What Rosa wants, Rosa gets. Or else my mother needs to find someone who will pay her a ridiculous salary to be at home and manage receipts."

"Max!" Rosalina shouts, and suddenly J.C.'s car door is pushed open from the inside.

"You still don't have to marry her," I whisper, and I get close enough to feel his breath. I know Rosalina can see our bodies pressed closer together, but I don't move regardless.

"I don't have to marry her. I probably won't, but it's going to get ugly before I'm free. I'm only preparing for the fallout and trying to make the break as gently as possible. But I'm trying to warn you. Don't get involved with Rosalina. There's always a catch."

I reach for the handle to J.C.'s door, and Max pulls my arm away and presses the door shut again. "I'm not done!" he snaps.

"It's a week. What could happen? There are plenty of NGOs building houses and looking for volunteers all the time. If it's endorsed by her office, all the better. Even Prince William and Kate worked in Chile. Not everyone has rules like Libby, and I can't be afraid to try again just because one thing failed."

Max keeps his hand pressed against the top of the door. "Go on vacation and leave this until you get home."

"Why are you so invested in what I do?"

"Because I have a bad feeling about this. About this *and* you. And I didn't want to tell you when I dropped you off at Libby's, but I felt the same way about you there."

"I can't say no." I try to explain further. "I've been too dependent. This is mine. I own it."

"Maybe the whole world's problems aren't yours. Your parents are adults. Let them take care of their own worries."

"Couldn't I say the same thing about you and being engaged?" It's not like Max has been the mountaintop of trust lately.

"Max?" Rosalina calls.

I tug at the door, and J.C. straightens his leg outward. Max helps him out and hands him his crutch. "Dude, I hope you get home."

"Thanks. I'll get you something for the car when I get home."

Max slides into the car without another word to J.C.

"I'm sorry about your car, Max," I say. "I know J.C. is too."

"Yeah, yeah."

I can see his forehead bead with sweat at the mere thought of getting a new vehicle.

"No, I'm going to do something to make it up to you. I promise. I'll talk to my parents."

He rolls his eyes at me. "Just go enjoy yourself at the hotel and forget about the car." He tries to take the manila envelope from me, but I clutch it to my chest.

"I won't do that!" I tell him, willing him to trust me. Willing him to accept help when he so clearly needs it. He needs to let that macho act go. "I can handle this."

Max shakes his head. "Does it ever occur to *you* to stop and take the help that's offered to you? I'm not talking about Rosalina's offer, you know. There's no rule that you have to do everything perfectly all the time, and you're so busy trying to fix my problem, you haven't noticed your own, which is in that innocent-looking envelope."

I hesitate. "Is this goodbye then?" I ask Max. "Will I see you again before I leave? Will I meet your mother?"

He says nothing, and then J.C. hovers over us.

"Can I get your information from Daisy? To pay for the car?" J.C. asks.

"Just forget about it." Max waves him off.

"I'm not going to forget about it. I take responsibility for my mistakes."

"Are you saying that I don't?" Max asks with his chest pumped outward.

"Max, don't be stupid. You need the help," I remind him.

"I don't need the help. You need the help, and you're so bound and determined to get that scholarship requirement done, you don't care who it hurts."

"How could it hurt to ask questions?"

He exhales. "Yeah, how could that hurt? Just forget about it. Forget about me. You've got Rosalina on your side now, and you've got your scholarship with J.C., so I guess everything is set for you. I'm sure if I should ever cross your mind, paying for a car isn't going to be on your list of priorities."

"Then you never really knew me." I take J.C.'s hand and bend back into the car. "Thank you, Rosalina, for the ride, for this information. You can't know how much I appreciate everything you've done. Max is a lucky man." It takes everything I have to keep the sarcasm from my voice.

She grins. "Just be there tomorrow and don't let me down."

"I promise," I tell her. "Wild horses, or whatever you have down here, couldn't drag me away."

As J.C. and I make our way to the gold glass doors of the hotel, it occurs to me I'm going to have a lot of explaining to do, and I'm not sure anything is going to meet my parents' standards.

J.C. stops at the doorway. "Maybe I should just take a taxi to the airport. I've imposed myself on you long enough."

"Without a flight? You can't sleep there all night if you can't get a flight."

"I don't want to meet your parents like this. Look at me."

Naturally, he still looks like J.C., so what exactly does he want me to say? He's suddenly heinous? "I don't think you have a choice. You can hardly go to the airport with no baggage or ticket looking like that. This is not the Greyhound bus station. I think you'll fare better with my parents than at the airport." I'm not entirely sure this is true, but I believe it's true, and right now that's enough.

He limps behind me to the elevator. "I'm sorry about Max, if it makes you feel any better. I didn't mean for any of that to happen."

"I'm sorry you picked my pathetic mission for your trip after seeing what I'd picked. Maybe if I'd known to warn you that I had the worst luck in the world, neither one of us would be in this situation."

"Why don't I come with you tomorrow to the NGO thing? I could help translate, and then I wouldn't feel like this entire trip was wasted."

"You need to get back home and get to your food bank, and I don't think they want a guy who looks like you on the pregnancy circuit of Argentina, if you know what I mean."

"Why not? There's little damage I could do if they're already pregnant."

I stare hard at him.

"It was a joke, Daisy. Lighten up."

"I can't lighten up. I keep thinking how I'm going to

explain your presence to my parents, but I can't let you go to the airport without a ticket either."

"I'll handle it. You haven't done anything wrong. Maybe you get in so much trouble because you automatically feel guilty, so everyone just assumes you're guilty."

"Maybe." I press the button to the floor where my parents are located and pray they're where they said they would be. It's going to be hard enough to explain my whereabouts all morning and afternoon. "I'm starving."

"We haven't eaten all day."

"Maybe we should go down to the restaurant and eat before we meet up with my parents. We could just put the tab on the room."

The elevator doors open. "Too late," J.C. says.

"I have to get a new travel journal. The napkins aren't doing the trick as journal paper. Why don't we hit the gift shop before we bother my parents? I bet they have some really nice ones down in the lobby. Did you see how nice their gift shop was? Don't you love how you can just buy anything in a gift shop? I mean, it's like this little mini everything store, and it's like they know exactly what you'll need and so they stock it. Even if you're only craving a candy bar. They have the best selection and—"

"Daisy, what room are your parents in?"

The door to their room opens unexpectedly, and my dad stands in the door frame right across from the elevator. He hasn't taken his eyes off J.C. since he opened the door. I have no time to regroup or plan my defense.

"Daisy."

"Hey, Dad."

"Who is this? What the heck happened to you, son?"

"Dad, this is J.C., and he was working with me at Libby's mission. And you know how you always told me that I should look out for the little guy and be a good Samaritan in all circumstances?"

"I have a feeling that's going to turn on me at the moment. Where's Max?" My dad comes out of the room and searches the hallway, as if Max has been on the elevator ahead of us.

"Max isn't here, Dad. Meet J.C.," I say as we step out of the elevator.

My dad brushes back what's left of his hair and finally reaches out his hand. "J.C., huh?" But naturally I'm getting the evil eye. Why does my dad give a perfect stranger the benefit of the doubt, while it's clear I'm going down sometime in the near future?

J.C. reaches out his good hand and awkwardly shakes my father's hand. "Nice to meet you, Mr. Crispin. I want to tell you how your daughter put her own scholarship in jeopardy to do the right thing, and most people would never do such a thing, so I think you've done an awesome job raising her."

"Do you now? Did Daisy have anything to do with all that you're wearing?"

"Not a thing. But she saved Libby from looking like this, and even though Libby will never know or appreciate it, your daughter did it anyway."

"At the expense of her scholarship, is that what you're telling me?" My dad glares at J.C., and I wish I could just crawl under the nearest rock, but no doubt a scorpion would be hiding out there and I'd look exactly like J.C. did. It's just that kind of trip.

"Yes, sir. But she took care of that too. She's arranged to start a new ministry tomorrow with a local NGO."

"Let's finish this conversation in the room, shall we?" My dad stretches across the door frame to let J.C. know in his own way that this may not be a comfortable situation. "Daisy, as you know, your mother and I had something to tell you. That's why we came out to the mission to begin with."

"Dad, can we talk about it after J.C. calls his grandmother and makes arrangements for his flight home?"

My mom stands beside my father. "What's going on?"

"Daisy has a friend with her."

"Daisy, we need to talk with you privately. That's why we came this morning."

"I know, Mom, but J.C. has to get home. He got stung by a scorpion and then a child abuser beat him up." I'm hoping that the child abuse thing makes them forget all about the fact that J.C. is (1) male and (2) someone I've known for three days in a foreign country.

"A child abuser?" My mom's eyes narrow.

"We had a little boy at the camp who kept wandering over alone with a bottle. No one with him at all. So J.C. was walking him home one afternoon, but J.C. got stung by a scorpion on the way back. I guess the little boy got scared."

"How does the child abuser come into this?" My mom has her arms crossed, and it's clear she doesn't believe even an inkling of the story. This is going to be harder than I thought.

"The little boy came back the next day, and we noticed he was bruised up, so we snuck him out to the medical clinic—"

"Why did you sneak him out? You should have told Libby. You two have no idea how things work down here, and you could have gotten into big trouble."

"Well, we sort of did, Mom. J.C. is beat up because he

didn't want to lead the boy's stepfather back to the mission and get Libby into trouble."

My mom looks at my father. "What do you think of all this?"

"I think we've always taught Daisy to stand up for the right thing, and today she did it. Along with her friend here. I'm proud of you, Daisy."

Did my father just say he was proud of me? When I nearly got arrested in a foreign country? I think I'm going to faint. But I realize it's too late because the next thing I know, J.C. is on the ground, laid into the designer carpeting. His broken arm is twisted up in a way that doesn't look good.

"Dad! Do something!"

My father assesses the situation, too slow for my tastes, and tells my mother to call the concierge and get help. "Have you two eaten today?" Dad looks up at me.

"I haven't, but he was in the hospital until this morning, so I assumed that he did. At least something."

My father grabs J.C.'s good wrist and checks his pulse. "His heartbeat is fine. Steady."

"Can we not play ER now? Do something."

"Daisy, go sit with your mother. You're far too emotional in these situations. He's going to be fine."

Says Dr. Crispin. And may I just say, a CPR class so you can perform skits in the local schools does not an expert make!

It's nearly dinnertime, and it's clear J.C.'s in no shape to go home for an umpteen-hour flight. "I need to call his grandmother again. She probably thinks he's on the flight home by now."

"Wait until he comes to," my father says. "You don't want to tell the old woman he's out cold and give her a heart attack. Go and get me some ice."

I do as I'm told, and I'm grateful my parents are here. After three days of handling crisis after crisis, it feels amazing to not have to think on my feet for a moment. I suppose I never fully appreciated that in my parents. They took the brunt of a lot of stuff for me, and it scares me that maybe I'm not ready to take the heat for my own life. In less than a month and a half, I will be in college, on my own, and responsible for getting myself fed, clothed, and educated, and suddenly that doesn't feel as freeing as it did a few days ago.

My mom hands me the ice bucket, and I run down the hallway until I hear the clank of an ice machine. I put the bucket under the lever and push, praying under my breath that this whole nightmare of a vacation will end as soon as possible.

"The concierge has contacted the on-call doctor," Mom says when I get back. "Until then, the concierge said not to move him."

"What about his arm? What if it's been knocked out of its place again?"

"The cast will hold it." My dad takes a bathroom towel my mother brought him and wraps some of the ice cubes inside it. He holds it to J.C.'s forehead, but he doesn't stir. "Is he diabetic?" my father asks. "Does he have insulin to inject?"

My eyes pop open. "I never thought of that, but you know, he was never without food in his backpack."

"Where's his backpack now?"

"It got stolen with the car."

"The what? Never mind. Honey, get me some juice out of the minibar. Did you see him with any kind of shot or insulin pump?"

I just shake my head, but in that magic bag of tricks he carried about, who knows what he had in there?

My mom runs to the minibar and fiddles with the key that's hanging from it for what seems an eternity. "Mom, hurry!" I run to the tiny fridge after she's opened it and look at the juices available. "Grape or bilberry?"

"Grape," my father announces without a pause. "Check if there's orange somewhere in there."

"Got it. Dad, what if he chokes?" I hand him the tiny bottle.

"Hold the towel under his head. If it's a diabetic coma, we're better off taking our chances."

As I watch my father try to pour orange juice into J.C.'s lax lips, I can only hope that's true.

17

My Life: Stop—July 9

Night—and the city is so beautiful!

As you can see, dear journal, I got myself a new travel journal. Maybe with it, I brought the hope that the rest of this trip will improve vastly.

I'd hoped this trip would be my foray into my new and independent world. That I would prove to my parents how over-parented I've been and that I'm capable—but it seems their version of me may be closer to the truth than I'd like.

Still, I'm proud of my parents and their ability to let go a little. They gave me their phone this morning, they didn't ask questions, and they trusted me to drive off into the wild blue yonder with Max Diaz. And . . . I ended up at the police station, and Max's car will probably end up in the scrap pile. Maybe I'm dangerous. Is that why my parents are overprotective? What if I'm not ready to be on my own and this failed mission trip is a marker? Maybe it's like God's pink slip—a notice that no, I'm not quite ready to be on my own.

Is that thought to protect me? In case my scholarship doesn't come through? I can't take my parents' money for college. They have scraped and scrimped their whole lives, and they've done their job. It's my problem now. I'm my own problem, not theirs.

I've had some quiet time. Spent time with the Lord while in the bathtub. I think the reception is better in the bathtub, personally. Maybe it's because I'm all exposed and can't really hide a thing at that point, but it's a place I feel at peace in prayer.

My dad went with J.C. to the local hospital. Let's be honest, I may have bad luck, but J.C. seems to medal in it. He wasn't diabetic, but severely hypoglycemic. My father was right with his treatment. Again.

What would I have done if J.C. had just passed out on me? What if I'd made him worse, or even killed him because I couldn't think of a better plan to get him to Buenos Aires? I can't imagine trying to explain to his grandmother that he was beaten to a pulp AND unfed, and I'd stood idly by while it all happened. That's a conversation I'll never have, praise God! My dad took that burden off me, which makes me feel all warm and cozy. Thank you, Daddy!!

J.C. is everything I dreamed about in a guy, but even as I write this, my thoughts stray to Max. J.C.'s a stand-up guy, willing to fight for "the weakest of these" like the Bible preaches, and as gorgeous as any actor you'll see in the latest iCarly episode. But there's a dark side, and I almost hate to admit how shallow and hypocritical I am here. But J.C. has incredibly bad luck. I mean, catastrophe follows him like the black dog of depression that Winston Churchill talked about. I realize how ironic this is, considering that if Claire had ever taken bad luck into account, I would never have acquired a best friend.

I suppose luck is not a godly concept or a fruit of the Spirit. The rain will fall on both the just and the unjust, right? We're supposed to reap what we sow, but what about when we don't? What about when we save an abused toddler from his evil stepfather and get rewarded by a stolen car, a broken arm, and a diabetic coma (okay, a hypoglycemic fainting spell)? Somehow it's not as hot, right? What about that? It's one of those questions I'll definitely have for God when I get my face-to-face. Along with why I had to wear homemade clothes at that elite private school. Did he think that improved my character somehow? Because I think it just left scars.

I mean, fine, make me born into a family who is crafty and creative and thinks making my clothes is a fine idea—but don't make me aware of it! I mean, couldn't I have been just like my parents and thought it was a cute and perfectly reasonable idea? Wouldn't that have made life much simpler?

This is something I'll be musing in my Argentina travel journal, since it doesn't look like I'll be doing much traveling. Though I will be asking young girls how they got pregnant. That ought to appeal to my mother and father. Just like the bandaged boy I brought back. I suppose it's not easy for my parents either. No doubt they wonder why they got me and not some earthy chick who liked to do gardening.

The good thing about all this chaos with J.C.'s sugar drop is that I haven't had time to process Max being pseudo-engaged. Or be obsessed about it, since it's clearly not my problem and there's nothing I can do to rescue him. He has to be his own hero. I have to be mine. Granted, with help from above, but there are those times that God feels so far away.

I said I wouldn't obsess, but I have to say that Rosalina is so beautiful, so who wouldn't feel self-conscious about having a crush on and a prom dance with Max? He told me he loved me. He said the words at graduation. Why would he do that if Rosalina was waiting?

I have to wonder if Max isn't right about her and her ulterior motives, but that's because I know Max. At least I think I do. What if what I feel about him in my gut *isn't true? What if he's just another dog like Chase, who only used me to feed his ego, not because he had any actual feelings for me?*

"Daisy! Are you still in there?" My mom knocks on the bathroom door. "Are you all right?"

"Yeah, Mom! Just writing in my journal in the tub."

"Dinner's going to be here soon. Maybe you should get out now."

"Be right there!" I call.

Back to NOT obsessing about Max. There are probably a lot of issues and history between Max and Rosalina, especially if their moms are involved. As much as I want to dislike her for being beautiful and being tied to Max, I can't let my jealousy taint my Christian view of her. She's involved in NGO work every day, so how can she not have a heart inside that 34D chest of hers?

I can't just assume that she's got all these evil intentions. That would be prejudice.

Prejudice is ignorance. Prejudice is ignorance. Prejudice against a pretty girl is ignorance.

Nope. Not working. Still don't like her.

I mean, Max isn't worth anything financially, and that can't be the ideal mate for an ambassador's daughter, so there's something he's not telling me. There have to be feelings on her part—and his? Maybe Max is taking out some misplaced anger about not going to college on poor

Rosalina. Maybe she has that body dysmorphic thing where she doesn't realize she's hot.

After all, it was so nice for Rosalina to find me a job when she could have just hated me (as, let's face it, I wanted to hate her). I'm sure she knows how Max can turn on the charm. He's probably aimed it at her many times, but as for me, I believed it. With my whole heart I believed that he was different. I wish I knew what it was about me that attracts the rats, but I seem to be giving off some kind of radio signal. It's definitely time that I changed my frequency because it's like a dog whistle: all I'm calling in are the hounds!

But yeah, even after all that, I still don't like Rosalina. Sorry, God. I'm doing my best, but you don't want me to lie, right?

More tomorrow after the new mission field. I like the sound of that: new mission field. There's so much hope in that phrase!

I come out of the tub and cinch the plush hotel robe around my waist. My journal is clutched in my pruned fingertips, and I feel cleansed inside and out. My mom is standing over the table filled with food she's ordered from room service, and I can hardly believe my mom has splurged on food brought to her. Normally she'd find the nearest grocery, borrow a hot plate somewhere, and cook something to save money. She is dressed in a form-fitting pencil skirt and heels with a wispy, scarf-like shirt.

"Mom, what are you wearing?"

She looks down. "Your father bought me this today in town. Isn't it gorgeous? I told him it was too extravagant, but he said that we only live once and plopped the money down on the counter. It was so manly."

"He bought you that outfit and the ring?"

"We were celebrating a gift God presented us with. Don't worry, we tithed first."

"I'm not worried. I'm just—you look beautiful, that's all. I'm not used to seeing you in clothes that show your shape."

"I didn't have much of a shape before."

"And you ordered room service. Are you sure you're my mom and not some alien imposter?"

She smiles to the point of dimples, then strides slowly toward the window. "We sold the business." She turns on her heel with her hand placed on her chest. "My business. That's what we came by to tell you this morning—that our money woes are over. You don't need the scholarship if you don't want to take it, and you certainly don't have to be mistreated by Libby. I know you have enough humility in you that you weren't rude to her. I didn't raise you that way."

"What?" I feel my breath leave me. "Back up. You sold the business? Our money woes are over? As in, we don't have to buy toilet paper in bulk, or we could afford to have it delivered if we ran out?"

"Sit down. I wanted to have a talk with you about something else first, so that you didn't take on the guilt of this failed trip."

I make my way to the lean, tufted gold sofa. "You've got to give me time to process that. You're rich?"

"We're rich. We made millions on the business. They bought the designs, the patterns, everything."

"Millions?" My mouth gapes open and I'm struggling to find breath.

"We won't live much differently, of course."

"Why the heck not?" I ask, musing on the massive storage unit our living room has become.

"Because that's not who we are. That's not what I wanted to discuss, though. We'll have plenty of time for that." She pats the sofa beside her.

"This isn't about today, is it? I made it back, and I promise you, neither Max nor J.C. tried a thing." *Not that this gives me bragging rights*, I want to add.

"No." Mom shakes her head. "I wanted to explain something I should have told you before I let you accept that assignment at Libby's mission. It's been bothering me increasingly since you left."

I think I may prefer ignorance, but my expression somehow encourages my mother.

"Libby had a crush on your father."

I was right. I shake my head. "That's enough. Don't need to tell me any more than that. Duly noted." I drop my journal beside me.

"I guess when I think back on it, she did everything she could to break us up in the singles' group we all belonged to."

"You didn't think I might have benefited from that kind of information before you sent me into the lion's den?"

"You're always so dramatic, Daisy. Truthfully, I'd forgotten all about it until I saw your face this morning. It reminded me of how much she intimidated me and made me feel unworthy of your father. When I saw that emotion on your face, I wanted to run in there and . . . what is it you and Claire say? Go ninja on her."

I laugh out loud at the idea of my mother going ninja on anyone. "Did she and Dad, you know, ever date?"

"No. Your father was out of college, and he was there in the dorms to see me, but she always managed to get him there alone somehow. Naturally, I started to question your father. I didn't know she had a crush on him. Someone on our floor told me that your dad kept arriving when I wasn't there, and he'd make haste and get out when Libby answered the door."

"No way!"

"I didn't think it was true until she started making excuses to be around when Dad would come and pick me up on campus after he caught on to her tricks."

"I thought she'd grow out of that stuff. Obviously, she got married."

"Most people throw that stuff aside. But Libby always was the sort to hold a grudge, and it doesn't look like she's given that up since your father married me. In a lot of ways, I don't think she even really liked your father. I think she was just in some invisible competition with me and I wasn't aware of it."

"I can believe that. But she's married to a perfectly nice man now."

"Oh, I know. We met him. He's wonderful. And I don't have any illusion that she regrets losing your father to me. It's that she just doesn't take losing well, no matter what the issue, and I'm sure this only reminded her of a loss. So I'm sorry if we put you in a precarious situation. I just heard 'Buenos Aires,' and I thought Libby was a way to keep you close and safe. My mistake."

I shake my head. "Well, I sure hope they take my paperwork from the embassy for my scholarship."

"That's what your dad and I came to tell you this morning. We thought you looked miserable there, and we thought about poor Claire giving up this lovely hotel when you both should be celebrating your accomplishment of graduating from high school. We wanted to make things right."

"I can't give up my scholarship just because you can pay for school, Mom. I worked hard for that, and it's mine."

Mom nods. "I understand, but now someone else who needs that scholarship can have it. We came to tell you that Kitchens Unlimited bought my business. We got the final agreement yesterday by fax at the hotel. I'm so grateful we were staying here. I doubt the dump we were in would have had a fax machine, much less a business office. That's why we agreed to this arrangement in the first place. The last thing we wanted to do was take charity from Claire's parents."

"It takes money to make money," I tell her.

"It really doesn't. I built that business from nothing, and the price they offered me . . ." She lowers her voice as though someone might overhear. "It was obscene!"

"You're saying I don't need my scholarship? I don't need to qualify for it this summer?" I'm trying to comprehend that life has just been handed to me on a silver spoon. I never get a silver spoon. I'm more of a plastic spork kind of girl.

"I feel terrible telling you such good news on such an awful day for you, but you should be grateful. I don't feel I did my job protecting you in regards to Libby, so you don't have to finish the mission."

"I do! Don't blame yourself, Mom. Besides, I promised Rosalina I'd be somewhere tomorrow to work with young pregnant girls doing research. It's ridiculous to throw away a scholarship for something so simple."

"Well, you can cancel it. Maybe even treat yourself to the

indoor pool or a spa treatment. Daisy, for once in our lifetimes we get to splurge. I know how serious you are about commitment, and I don't want you to think I don't appreciate that. But I'm worried maybe you've forgotten how to have fun. Maybe you don't make enough time for joy in your life like other kids."

"I don't want to splurge. I earned that scholarship and I'm taking it. I'm not letting someone like Libby defeat me. I'm going to finish this."

"But someone else who might not be able to afford school could benefit—"

"Mom, I'm not taking chances with my education. It's all I have going for me, and I earned that scholarship fair and square."

"You have a lot going for you, Daisy. You're a beautiful girl. You have a best friend who takes you on a trip like this and then works during it to help you. You have job experience, and you're so good with money. What you don't have is the ability to stop and let God lead."

"That's not true. Yes, I'm good with money, and I don't intend to start spending it like there's no tomorrow because your business got bought. Mom, you and Dad are so talented and I'm so thrilled for you both, but this whole trip was about my independence. I've been independent for three days and now you're telling me I don't need to be."

"What about us? This is our chance to be the kind of parents that all your friends have."

"I don't want those kind of parents. I want the kind of parents who scrape by so they can accompany me to Buenos Aires so I don't get hurt. Parents who don't care what the Joneses have because they feel passionate about teen abstinence and make fools of themselves doing a rap at their daughter's high school."

"You handled yourself fine. So it's proven. No need to go out and prove yourself further. Sometimes we need to know when to stop." Mom crosses her legs. "I never see you stop. God says to be still and know he is God. When do you sit still?"

"I just sat still. To the point of pruning in the bathtub."

"Without a journal. Without a plan for your future. I mean sitting. Still. Listening."

I stand up and pace the busy carpet. "I need to be independent. I still count on you, don't you see? I knew you would be here for me. I knew I could run back to the hotel at any time. I just have to do the requirements because I promised to do them. Does that make sense?"

"Not a bit. God's there for you. He'll always be there for you, but I'm worried your faith is running more on the belief system of Daisy Crispin than it is on God."

"God helps those who help themselves." I cross my arms in front of me as if I've won some kind of battle.

"Ben Franklin said those words. Not God. You, Miss Fact Checker, should know that more than anyone."

"I can't stop, Mom. If I stop . . ." My voice starts to crack. "If I stop, I'll have to think about how Max is just another guy who broke my heart. I'll have to think about how I failed at Libby's and how I didn't do the one small requirement asked of me for the scholarship. I'll have to stop and dwell on all my failures."

"Then that's just what you need to do, because I don't care how perfectly you think you've done anything—you're flawed. This is my whole point. The more you rely on your own perfection, the more God will show you it's his you need to rest upon. Are you prepared for that?"

I have no quick answer for her question, and I have the urge to escape the fancy suite and run away. If this kitchen company comes through, I'll be more than happy to take the money and give the scholarship to someone else. But if it doesn't—my family is not known for its business acumen—then I'm covered. But I don't want to say that in front of my mom and let her believe I doubt my parents.

My mom goes on. "So how long will you fight for your so-called independence? What if God is trying to say it's time to let your guard down and rely on others?"

"I did that, and look where it got me—in jail with Max's car stolen. Not to mention J.C. passed out. That's what community got me."

Mom shakes her head. "No, that's what trying to micromanage got you. You could have let J.C. handle his own problem. You could have let Libby know she was in danger rather than protect her with ignorance. You made those decisions, Daisy. You played God."

I stand up and walk to the table of food near the window. I shove a roll into my mouth rather than find an answer.

"I thought you'd be happier than anyone about the sale of my business. You with your love of store-bought clothes and having followed Claire around the country club all those years, and having worked for spoiled Gil with that revved-up sports car of his. I couldn't wait to tell you of all people, but you want to throw it back at me and work for a scholarship you don't need. I don't understand that."

"Mom." I swallow the roll and grab her hands, which are soft and manicured. "I couldn't be happier for you and Daddy.

No one deserves success like you two. You've dedicated your whole life to what you believe in. When Daddy got sick, you came in and rescued the day with your talent. I'm so proud of you, but I want to feel that same sense of accomplishment. Do you understand that?"

"No, because you've had to work for everything up until now, unlike your friends. You've had to watch them have great success while you worked for it. I want you to know what that feels like for a change."

I almost can't believe that came out of her mouth, but I've seen what having money has done for my friends. They've succeeded in college applications because that's what is expected of them, not because they have their own drive. I'm worried if I suddenly have things handed to me, I won't remember how to work for them and I'll be dependent forever.

Still, I want to know that the money truly exists. *Show me the money!* If for any reason, Mom is a tad too optimistic and I haven't completed my scholarship requirements, I'll be living in the realm of excess toilet paper in my parents' garage forever. That's a chance I cannot take.

My mom stands and walks closer to the window, where she perches herself on the golden paisley chair with its elegant Queen Anne legs and rests her chin on her hand. "I hadn't thought about you wanting to do it alone. I guess that makes me nervous. How will you share your life with someone if you think you have to do everything alone?"

"It's like all those chastity talks you had with me, Mom. It didn't mean much unless I'd made that decision for myself."

Her eyes grow huge.

"And of course, I did make that choice for myself, Mom."

"Don't scare me like that. The longer you fight and avoid

relaxing into what God has for you, the more I worry. Faith should be like a beautiful downhill ski run, not a clumsy climb uphill in cross-country gear."

"Maybe my faith is sloppy—too reliant on myself. But I'm not sure I know how to let go of the reins, or that I can trust God if I do."

We both gasp.

And there you have it, Mom is right again.

18

In the morning, I wake up in the luxury golden bed under a mound of a down feather comforter. It dawns on me that I feel no better waking up in the suite than I did in the cement cabin. My mind still worries about the day's events and I'm without peace. Will I need my scholarship? Won't I? Will Max explain his betrayal to me? Or won't he?

I feel guilty for enjoying this plush life in six-hundred-thread-count sheets while Claire lives my own life in the coldhearted mission of misery.

I'm enjoying the Argentine sunshine streaming through the windows, and since the sun hasn't been shining too much since I arrived in the southern hemisphere, I can only assume this is a good sign. My parents are in the suite's attached bedroom, and apparently J.C. is sleeping on the sofa. I'm sure the hotel management thinks the Simpsons have come to life and are currently staying in a luxury suite overlooking the infamous cemetery.

Sleeping in was a delight, but then there's a knock on the door. I wonder if my parents have ordered breakfast at some ungodly hour, but I hear someone speaking in English and

I realize I'd better get dressed quickly. I climb into the only pair of clean jeans I have left, don a bright pink sweater, and twirl a scarf around my neck so I appear cosmopolitan and not simply an American teenager. I slather my face in tinted sunscreen (i.e., makeup that's mother-approved) and enter the main salon of the suite.

Max is there, dressed in black jeans, a silky, red-collared shirt, and black dress shoes. Let's just say it's not an outfit one could pull off in America, but here he looks as natural as if he were the lead in *Dancing with the Stars*.

"Max, what are you doing here?"

"Come sit down," my father tells me.

"Where's J.C.?"

"He's still sleeping," my mother answers.

My father holds the manila envelope with my instructions for the day.

"Dad, what are you doing with that?" I reach for the envelope, and he lifts it above his head like I'm five years old.

"Did Max tell you not to sign up for this ministry?"

"He did, but he had ulterior motives, so I didn't listen. It's his fiancée who gave me the packet. Did he tell you that?"

"He did," my father says.

I scowl at Max, but he stares out the window rather than man up and face me. Tattletale.

"Didn't your mother talk to you yesterday about being still in the Lord?" Dad asks.

"Yes, but—"

"Did you pray about this ministry?"

"No, but I didn't really have time. Rosalina had the envelope and I didn't want to let the opportunity get away from me, so I grabbed it."

"Even after Max told you he had reservations about it."

"Dad, he—"

"Part of being independent is knowing who to trust when you're in an uncertain situation. Since you're in a foreign country and know little about the customs or the rules here, I would think you would automatically defer to your friend Max, who knows the lay of the land."

"Yes, Dad."

"You need to call this Rosalina person and tell her you will not be there as promised."

"But Dad, let your yes be yes and your no be no."

"Be as wise as serpents and gentle as doves," he says back to me. "Abortion is illegal in Argentina, did you know that?"

"No," I answer.

"Only with a lot of paperwork and distinct rules is it available here, and these questions are to mine information and tell young women there is an easier way for them than going through labor and parenting."

"I didn't know."

"But Max did, and next time when you're in Buenos Aires, I expect you to listen to him."

"Yes, sir."

"You are always so headstrong, Daisy, but sometimes you need to know when to ask for help and find a way other than brute force."

"Can I go now?"

"No, Max is here for a reason. Max?"

"I feel bad that you didn't get your prom in the States, so my church is putting on a formal tonight," Max tells me. "Claire will be back, and if J.C. is up to it, he can come too. But I want you and Claire to wear the gowns your mother bought and come with me so Buenos Aires can show you a proper good time."

"Gowns?" I look toward my mom and she nods. "What about Rosalina? Isn't that the real reason I didn't get my proper date?"

"I've told my mother, Rosalina's mother, and Rosalina that enough is enough. We'd be unequally yoked, and I still plan a life in ministry. She wants to marry a foreign head of state. I want to work for the Lord. Over dinner last night, that was the final straw—the fact that I had no aspiration for a 'real' job. She freed me from my bond, and she's off to find love in a wealthier, more stable place, I'm certain."

I look at my parents, and they're both grinning and nodding their heads.

"I knew I was right about you, Max, but you do try a girl's soul," I say.

"I believe I've heard those words before." Dad smiles.

"And for once you're not in complete control," my mother says. "Think you can handle that? Just having fun for a night?"

"I do."

19

"You look different," I tell Claire when she arrives back at the suite.

"I feel different. I feel as though I found my purpose here. I love kids. Did you know that?" she asks me.

I shake my head.

"I didn't know it either, but I do. I love them. I love their honesty and their raw ability to love and seek the connection they desire. It's the first time I've felt alive in years."

"So what does that mean?"

"It means I'm not coming back home with you. You'll be off at college, as will all our friends, and that's just not for me. At least not yet. I'm going to stay here and learn the ropes from Libby. Then I'll see where God leads me." Claire cinches the taffeta belt on her electric-blue frock.

"It's very Kate Middleton."

"I can't believe your mother picked it out."

"I think she had help. She didn't grow taste overnight." I smack my forehead. Why can't I think sweet thoughts like my mother does? Shouldn't it be genetic or something?

"Yours is very elegant," Claire tells me.

I twirl in the full-length mirror in the bathroom and watch

the fabric ebb and flow in the air. My dress is pale pink with tiny rhinestones lining the skirt's hem, so when I turn, it floats like a cloud behind me. "This whole day feels like a dream, as though it can't be happening."

"A lot more of these dreams might happen if you weren't so annoyingly rigid about planning every second."

"Thanks."

"Max will be here soon. He said that the dances here are much more social, much less romantic and one-on-one. Think you can handle that?" Claire asks.

"For once, I think I can. Where has my undying devotion to a guy ever gotten me?"

"Let's see, the principal's office, the police station, and Buenos Aires."

"From now on, I'm devoted to life with one man." I point up to the ceiling. "Anyone else is going to have to tirelessly apply for my devotion and wait on his answer."

"I hope that's true."

"Me too," I tell her honestly. Claire has made my eyes up like a cat with navy sparkle eyeliner and fake eyelashes. I'm not certain what my mother will think, but I feel like a cow with these extensive lashes, as if my eyes are headlights one cannot miss.

There's a knock at the door, and Claire and I look at one another. "Think this will be anything like prom?" Claire asks.

We both giggle.

"No, I think it will be better," I say. "A thousand times better."

"At least," Claire agrees.

As we open the bathroom door and enter the salon, J.C. is resting on the sofa with his leg straightened on the coffee table. He looks like a million bucks cleaned up, and he wobbles to a standing position at the sight of us. "You two look incredible! Who would have thought you could look anything like this?"

"Is that a compliment?" Claire asks him.

"It is, actually. Your camping selves were hiding all this."

"I'll get the door," my mother sings as she bursts through the room, but she halts at us. "Look at you two. Don't you look beautiful! Beautiful!"

My father claps, and I can't help but roll my eyes.

"Don't do that. They'll get stuck that way," my mother says. "Honey, get the camera so we can get pictures."

My dad grumbles but produces a camera within moments. As I open the door, Max is immediately blinded by a flash. "Wow, hi." He feels out in front of him. "Are my dates here? I'm too blinded to see." Max has two corsages in clear plastic boxes.

"They're here," J.C. answers. "But you only get one of them. I may be crippled, but I intend to dance Argentine style." He makes some awkward movement and we all burst into laughter.

"I'll explain to my friends that that's a dance move and not an epileptic fit," Max says. "One for you." He hands me the corsage, a mixture of pink roses and baby's breath. "And one for you," he says to Claire.

We slide them onto our wrists, and I feel as if this makes up for all the dark days of high school, all the times I didn't fit in and it felt like no one cared. Today I am in my best store-bought dress. I am wearing strappy, silver kitten heels, and my hair is pinned up in a lovely rhinestone crown that matches the skirt of my dress. I feel like a true princess, a daughter of the King, and I'm so grateful that tonight is a surprise. I didn't have time to set my expectations too high, so I can only be impressed.

After we pose for what seems like an entire yearbook's worth of pictures, the four of us head downstairs to the waiting limousine. "After you," Max says, holding out his arm. He helps me into the limo, then takes Claire's hand and does the same thing. Finally, he assists J.C. in, and we're all mesmerized by the lights lining the inside of the vehicle and awed by the gadgets in the vast backseat.

My father is still behind us snapping pictures when we enter the car, as if we're stars trying to break free from the paparazzi. When the door shuts, I breathe a sigh of relief.

When we arrive at the church, there are small lights strewn all around the entrance like we're about to enter a magical fairy tale. American music blares from within the small, quaint building, and teens dressed in their best gowns and suits dance away to the beat of the song.

"It looks like the party has already started!" I yell at Max over the music.

"It's not every day we get a party thrown for us like this. Look at the spread of food over there." Max points to the corner where a row of tables is set up and covered in red tablecloths. The food tables are manned by several caterers, and the smell of barbecued steak fills the air. I breathe in deeply and try to take in the entire picture, which is more than I ever could have imagined for prom back home.

Swaths of fabric are elegantly draped from the ceiling. Tiny, sparkling lights hang in a magical canopy, and my senses are alive with all the brightly colored gowns, the suit-clad guys, and the mixture of delicious scents from cologne to grilled shrimp. I hardly know where to look first, but the thumping beat from a CeLo song gives way to a slow tune. Ironically, the song's name is "Marry Me."

"Is it safe to dance this song with you?" I ask Max.

"Scout's honor. I'm not marrying anyone until I'm done with divinity school and have a parsonage of my own."

"Fair enough." I take his hand and he holds me close as we enter the crowded dance floor. "Your church sure puts on a spectacular dance."

"Your parents did this."

I stop dancing. "My parents did what?"

"Arranged for this dance. It's Sunday night, and we don't usually have dances on Sunday night. And we never have the kind of food you'd find in a tourist restaurant."

"Why would my parents do this?"

Max starts to sway to the music again, and though we're arm's length apart now, I feel pulled into the rhythm. "Because they wanted to show you grace. They felt maybe you'd learned all about God's rules, but not as much about his grace. Did you notice the theme of the dance when we came in? 'Grace Covers All.' It was your mom's idea."

"Apparently, her company really did get bought." I stare over at J.C., who is hobbling around the dance floor with Claire, and I'm struck by the grace I've received thus far from my parents. From Claire. From Max. From J.C. So why do I always look to the people who don't extend it to me, like Libby? Why do I dwell on the negative and look for places God isn't, instead of where he is?

"Do you mind if we get something to eat?" I ask.

"Not at all."

I scan the scene in front of me and can hardly believe my

parents had anything to do with this, much less pulled it off in what had to be a very short time. Unconditional love is incredible. I don't think I've ever felt so enveloped in warmth and the grace of others. Maybe it's been my attitude the entire time. Maybe if I'd been less concerned with doing things my way and getting away from my parents' way of life, I might have seen the wonderful aspects of their spiritual gifts all along.

"My parents really are incredible," I say as Max hands me a plate for the buffet. "Did you know they arranged for J.C. to fly home with us so he could get help if he needed it?"

"I know they're very unselfish people, and they always put your interests first."

"Are you trying to make me feel guilty?"

"Heck, no. I'm trying to make you see where you get it from."

I put my plate back down. "I'm not so hungry after all."

Max sweeps me back onto the dance floor, and we tango, slow dance, salsa, and everything in between (though I think no professional would call any of the dances I did by their professional name) until the lights dim to announce a break for the DJ.

"This vacation has been nothing like I expected, and yet everything I needed."

"That's how God works."

We find a round table and sit beside J.C. and Claire, who are both sampling food like they haven't been fed in the last two weeks. I think about all the years I was so jealous over Claire and her parents, only to see her give it all up for a fraction of the acceptance my parents have shown me.

"We're going to be apart for the first time." I grasp her hand.

"But we'll both be where we belong, and you know what I'm thinking anyway. Do you really need to hear it from me?"

I laugh. "Probably not." I rest my head on Max's shoulder, then switch to the other side and rest it on J.C.'s shoulder. "I'm so grateful for you all!" I shout this just as the last song ends, and Claire looks right at me and bursts into a fit of laughter over my obvious lack of the cool factor.

For once in my life, I don't feel like I need a boyfriend. I feel like my life is pretty good, and romance, when it's time, will come. For now I'm just happy to be in the present. To bask in the day God has made for me and to practice letting him take the reins.

He's made my life perfectly ridiculous. Having really good friends to laugh with through the absurdity is just icing on the cake. And I for one wouldn't have it any other way.

Acknowledgments

Thank you to my wonderful team at Revell. Lonnie Hull DuPont, you make writing feel like such a dream when I get to editing. Thank you so much for all of your efforts, kind words, and corrections. Donna Hausler, thank you for handling all those details! Janelle Mahlmann, thank you for keeping me on track and providing all those great marketing materials that make my job so much easier. Karen Steele, Jessica English, and Sheila Ingram, thank you for making this book come together and for getting the word out!

Kristin Billerbeck is the bestselling author of several novels, including *What a Girl Wants* and *Perfectly Dateless*. A Christy Award finalist and two-time winner of the American Christian Fiction Writers' Book of the Year, Kristin has appeared on the *Today Show* and has been featured in the *New York Times*. She lives with her family in Northern California.

Meet

Kristin Billerbeck

Visit her website at www.kristinbillerbeck.com

Read her blog at girlygirl.typepad.com/girly_girl

Friend her on Facebook

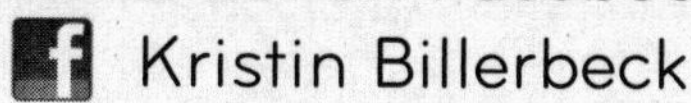

Kristin Billerbeck

Follow her on Twitter

KristinBeck